Buddha's Wife

A Novel

Gabriel Constans

Robert D. Reed Publishers   ●   Bandon, OR

Robert D. Reed Publishers
P.O. Box 1992
Bandon, OR 97411
Phone: 541-347-9882 • Fax: -9883
E-mail: 4bobreed@msn.com
web site: www.rdrpublishers.com

Cover Designer: **Cleone L. Reed**
Editor: **Kate Rakini**
Interior Designer: **Barbara Kruger**

ISBN 978-1-934759-29-5

Library of Congress Control Number 2009922690

Manufactured, typeset and printed in the United States of America

Mixed Sources
Product group from well-managed forests and other controlled sources
www.fsc.org Cert no. SW-COC-002283
© 1996 Forest Stewardship Council
FSC

Dedication

In honor of Yasodhara, Ambapali, Pajapati, Chitra, Maudenka, Pchiti, Visakha and all women throughout history who have been minimized, ignored or solely remembered as an appendage to their family or spouse. Bless you all for your wisdom, strength, courage and unrelenting compassion. Without you, we would not be. Without you, there is no path, no way, no enlightenment nor peace. Without you, there is no story.

Acknowledgments

With deep gratitude to Shona, Jason, Darcy, Marko, Leti, Wendy and Brendon for teaching me how to be a good father; Charmiel Teresi, for her faith; Santa Cruz, for grounding me in home and community; bell hooks, Isabel Allende, Alice Walker and Steven Levine, for waking me up; Marcy Alancraig, for inspiring countless writers, including this humble scribe; Elaine Cashman, for her enduring friendship; Bob Reed for following his gut; Cleone L. Reed for her keen eye and clarity; Kate Rakini for her masterful pen; and Audrey, for her tender strength and loving heart.

One

I barely made it to the corner bucket, relieved myself, and crawled back to the cot when Ananda entered the doorway with his old arms straining to hold a few pieces of scrawny firewood.

I've been getting by for several full moons in this small, but more than adequate, hut on the outskirts of Rajagaha, the capital of Magadha. Rajagaha was the first city my husband Siddhartha visited when he snuck off in the middle of the night and left us (his son and me) at his father's palace in Sakya. This is the last place I thought I'd be dwelling, but my best friend and cousin Kisa Gotami, the niece of Siddhartha's father, lives close by. She insisted I come, "where I can keep an eye on you," and said I could stay here as long as needed. Kisa's brother Devadatta and his family have also moved into Rajagaha, as have many villagers over the last five decades.

Kisa came yesterday afternoon and stayed until morning, when she returned to care for her own family. Kisa was widowed with two daughters, Radha and Retna, until she broke the taboo of remaining faithful to one's husband, whether he is dead or alive, and married Davidia, a silk merchant in Rajagaha.

She had been forced to leave her parents and marry elsewhere, which had been no small sacrifice. She and I had both been raised as princesses and were expected to become queens of our respective clans. Her father, King Bishanara, and the other men in the village have not spoken to her since, but her mother Lasha has made several secret trips to see her daughter and grandchildren.

"Ananda?" I pulled the blanket to cover my shoulders.

He nodded and put the wood down by the circle of rocks, where Kisa had started a small fire in the evening to keep the chill of the coming rainy season at bay. She had to stand by the fire and fan the smoke out the front door until the rocks were heated.

Ananda hobbled over to the night bucket and took it outside. I heard the scuffling of his feet along the path, then a splash of liquid falling on the dry earth. He returned and placed the covered bucket back in the corner, then sat cross-legged by the side of the bed.

As I looked at his aging face, I recalled the story Kisa had heard about a woman named Pakati who had her eye on Ananda when he was a young monk. Pakati was of the Matanga caste and had met him at a well by her village. Ananda, passing by, no doubt on some errand for Siddhartha, asked her if she would get him some water to drink. She replied that she couldn't because of her caste, and Ananda said, "I ask not for caste but for water."

It was the first time anyone had looked past her caste and seen her as a human being. After quenching his thirst, he thanked her and left. Unbeknownst to him, she was following not far behind, and even though he wouldn't admit it, he couldn't stop thinking of her either. He could still smell her fragrance and see her beautiful smile as he walked hurriedly, head bowed in contemplation, along the dusty road.

After following Ananda for some distance, Pakati began to inquire from other villagers as to his identity. She was told that he was a disciple of Gotama Sakyamuni, the Buddha, and that he was staying in the next province. She returned home at dusk and told her parents that she was leaving to become a disciple of the Buddha. They were appalled. She was only sixteen. Ananda was about twenty at the time. They refused and said only rich Brahmins with wealthy parents go off on such flights of fancy. She argued late into the night, but neither she nor they budged. Her mother found her bed empty the next morning and immediately set out after her daughter after learning where Gotama of the Sakyas was residing.

When Pakati reached the crowds surrounding Siddhartha, she pushed her way through, told him about Ananda's actions at the well, and said, "Great Teacher, please let me live with your disciple Ananda and minister unto him the rest of his days, for I love him with all my heart and soul."

Ananda, off on another errand, didn't hear about Pakati's request until he returned. Siddhartha never personally told him of the girl's plea and proclamation of love and devotion.

Siddhartha told Pakati, "You do not understand yourself. What you call love is but kindness. You don't love Ananda. You are attracted to his human kindness. Go, with the humility of your station in life, and practice the kindness you received from Ananda with others."

Pakati was devastated. Not only had she been rebuked for her love, but she'd also been told to stay in her place, in her "station." Her mother had found her at the edge of the crowd, sobbing in the dirt. Feeling broken, betrayed, and discounted, she returned home. Years later she, like me, joined other women followers of Siddhartha to be as close to her love as possible and to find inner peace.

I've tried to talk with Ananda about love, but he freezes. His shoulders tighten into hardened knots and his lips squeeze together like figs. He, like Siddhartha, is afraid of desire. He believes that desire, attachment, and human love are the cause of suffering.

He and Siddhartha didn't comprehend the shame their teaching and way of life had brought upon the thousands of women who have been left alone to fend for themselves. How could we explain to our relations and elders, let alone ourselves, why our men had left us for some elusive concept of happiness? Weren't we good enough? Had we done something wrong? Were we offensive in some way?

"So," Ananda said quietly, looking in my direction, but not in my eyes, "Sister, tell me your thoughts."

"Sister? I'm no longer in the order, remember?"

"Tell me," he continued, as if I hadn't spoken. "Tell me of your life."

"Well…" I looked up at the ceiling. "Sure you want to hear this?" From the corner of my eye I saw that his attention had not wavered.

I decided to give in to his daily requests about my past and began. "I was born in Klipati, in the foothills of the Himalayas. My father's family name was Suprabuddha. My mother was Chityananda. I have a brother, Devadatta, who is still living, and a twin sister, who died soon after birth.

"My family was wealthy, as my father was King of that province. I grew up with servants, garments of silk from Benares, and more than enough food, even in times of disasters and famines.

"I had no idea what it was like for the rest of the village. There were hard times, but I knew nothing of it. My mother and father kept me inside the palace grounds and everyone who attended to us had to pretend to be happy, even if they hadn't eaten in days or a family member had just died."

Ananda's eyes softened.

"My favorite attendant was Jihan. She was like a second mother to Devadatta and me. She always knew where we were and what we had been doing. She also knew when to show us a little tenderness and when to scold us and let us know who was in charge. I'd talk to Jihan when I needed advice or comfort.

"I remember I must have been about five or six at the time when Devadatta and his friends called me a long-nosed elephant. I was devastated. I went running to my room crying like a hyena. Everyone in the house heard me, but Jihan was the only one who came to my side to find out what had happened."

I turned towards Ananda and put my head on my folded hands. "I was so upset; it must have sounded like monkey gibberish. I doubt she understood a word I said, but it didn't matter. She put her arm around my shoulders, stroked my head, and said, 'Boys can be cruel, my little princess.' She was the only one who ever called me princess. 'Believe it or not,' she said, 'one day you'll like them so much, you'll forget about their meanness.'

"'Never!' I'd shouted through my sobs. 'I hate boys!'

"Of course, she was right. By the time I was eleven, I thought boys were living jewels. They had all the privileges and none of the responsibilities that I saw the women of the house burdened with. They made decisions, made the laws, and had the power. I wanted to be like them. I wanted to have some control over what happened. But it was futile. We were treated like property and were excluded from any exterior life. The laws and codes that my family and most of those in the area followed were beyond abominable."

My eyes focused on Ananda. "And don't tell me times have changed for the better. You know better than anyone how adamant Gotama was about not allowing us into the order. If it wasn't for your intercession, we'd still all have been seen as inferior, inhuman, as beings not able to attain the same enlightenment that men seek."

Ananda closed his eyes and smiled. He thought about the time when he, the Buddha, and their followers had set out for Vesali, the capital of Videha. Vesali is on the northern banks of the Ganges River. Siddhartha's father's widow, Pajapati Gotami, who was the Buddha's aunt and stepmother, had cut her hair, put on filthy clothes, and followed the Buddha to seek membership in their order. Gotama had refused her pleas three times before Ananda had come upon her weeping in her yellow robe. She had walked all day and night from Kapilavatthu. Her feet were swollen and cracked. She had explained to Ananda why she was in such a state, and he had promised to personally intercede on her behalf.

"You sly old fox," I interrupted his recollection. "You set the right bait." An imperceptible grin graced the corners of his wrinkled mouth.

I remember him telling me that Siddhartha, Pajapati's stepson, had been sitting on a large flat stone, instructing a number of new followers in the Eightfold Path. Uncharacteristically, Ananda interrupted him and asked point blank, "Great Teacher, are animals and all living things capable of becoming fully awake?"

Siddhartha said, "Yes, Ananda, they are."

Then he asked, "Are women capable of becoming stream-enterers and attaining enlightenment?"

Siddhartha replied, "Yes, they are, Ananda."

"Would it not then be a good thing to ordain Pajapati and the other women who have come to find the Way?" Ananda asked.

Siddhartha, realizing he had been trapped, smiled and said, "Yes, Ananda. Pajapati and the other women should be admitted as nuns, but they will have to follow strict guidelines. As you know, it is a hard life."

"Thank you. I will go tell Pajapati of your excellent decision to allow them into the Sangha," Ananda replied.

"You may not thank me in the future, Ananda," Siddhartha said. "I am afraid that women will be a great blight upon the order."

Ananda said that that was one of his happiest days. He played it like a game, seeing how often he could get his way with Siddhartha. It also meant that he would be able to be near me, since he had seen me in the company of Pajapati. He'd become aware of my presence years ago, when Siddhartha had returned to Sakya and visited family.

"How I miss Jihan," I continued, remembering her fierce devotion. "She was such a gift. The day after I turned fifteen, my mother and father came to my room. Father said, 'Yasodhara, we have arranged for you to be married.' His eyes were lit up like a lantern, but I froze, having no idea who it could be. 'We have chosen Siddhartha of Gotama.' My mother beamed. I sighed with relief, jumped in the air, and threw my arms around their waists. 'Yes! Thank you!' I shouted. I had dreamed of Siddhartha but never thought he would be mine.

"As soon as my parents had pried themselves away, Jihan, who had been listening from behind the drapes, rushed in and almost smothered me with hugs and kisses.

She was the first to share my joy. You would have thought she was getting married by her infectious glee. I never had anyone fuss over me as much as she did. Day after day, week after week, she seemed to never sleep."

Tears dripped down my cheek, over my hands, and onto the pillow. "Between her and my mother...I was the luckiest girl in the world. They flattered, pampered, and seduced me with expectations of eternal happiness. Nothing would be as wonderful as marrying the handsome, divine prince Siddhartha! 'Surely,' they'd insisted, 'He will supply your every need and give us healthy sons and grandsons to raise and adore.'

"They would come chattering into my room early in the morning and insist that I start my yoga practice, 'for your posture' they said, then bathe me in oils and perfume in order to 'please the senses of my husband and his family.'

"And my hair! They shampooed, combed, and brushed my dark black hair from the top of my head down to my waist a thousand times between sunrise and sunset. 'Your hair is a symbol of your beauty,' they insisted, 'And to attract and hold onto your man with your beauty is your power, your right, and your gift.'"

I turned on my back, closed my eyes, and smoothed out my long, now gray hair over the pillow. Before falling into a sound sleep I heard Ananda's joints creaking as he arose. He reached over, touched my hair, and quietly left.

Two

Kisa slipped in quietly as dusk fell. She stored the food she'd brought in her basket and was just putting the lid on the well water she'd poured into the jug when I awoke.

"Ananda, is that you?" I asked, without looking at the silhouette leaning over the earthen pot.

"No, my sweet," Kisa said, as she came to my bed. "It's just me, Kisa."

"Just you?" I admonished.

"Yes, just me."

I reached up and pulled her to me. We embraced.

Kisa had been fanatically jealous when she'd heard about my betrothal to Siddhartha. She called me every foul, dirty name she could spout, and on one occasion tried to pull out my hair. She had been intoxicated, as had many women, with Siddhartha's beauty, wealth, and presence and had vowed at an early age to make him her own. Even though we had been best friends, as well as cousins, since attending traditional dance classes together at age four, Kisa refused to speak to me throughout the winter and spring of my engagement.

But when Siddhartha left us, Kisa was the first to arrive and hold me in her arms. She had apologized earlier in the year and told me about her jealousy and fear that she would never find someone as wonderful as Siddhartha. But in the months between my marriage and Siddhartha's leaving, Kisa had been betrothed to Prince Krishnabathi, another Sakyan clansman, from her mother's side of the family. Her engagement to a well-respected aristocrat, whom she had discovered wasn't bad looking and seemed to be attracted to her round face, full bottom, and broad shoulders, had taken some of the sting out of her anger towards me, which, of course, was really directed at Siddhartha for not choosing her.

A raggedy goat entered the hut and headed for the food Kisa had placed on the table.

"Oh no you don't, you sneak, you," Kisa admonished, as she chased the nosey creature out the front door, stooping low so as not to knock herself out on the sagging beam.

She came back in and complained, "Why don't you go back home or come live with us?"

"You know I am not welcome in my father's house," I said, holding myself up on one elbow and rubbing my eyes. Kisa lit the candle that sat on the rocks by the fire and placed it on the narrow nightstand by my bed. "You know that after my parents died my relatives insisted that I live the ascetic life I'd chosen. It doesn't matter that I've left the order."

"Yes, yes," Kisa shook her head, "as if I didn't know," and sat on the side of the bed.

I thought about her parents, especially her father and how incensed he'd been when she had left home, re-married, and become a lay disciple of Siddhartha. He had refused to come to her wedding and hadn't spoken to her in twelve years. He'd never even met his own grandchildren!

"But surely as the sun rises, you know you are welcome in our home," Kisa said. "The children are almost grown and we all adore you." She placed her hand on my chest as I put mine on hers.

"I have never doubted your friendship or your love, but this practice of dying must be mine and no one else's to bear. And...my Rahula will surely be returning any day." I could feel myself holding my son again. Nothing else could bring such peace. "But thank you, Kisa. Thank you with all my heart for all our years as sisters of the Way."

"You're as stubborn as ever," Kisa exclaimed, as she went to fetch a cup of water. "Remember the day you and Siddhartha were betrothed? You insisted I be your maid of honor, even though you knew I was a jealous beast." Kisa returned with the water, placed it in my shaky hands, then sat at the end of the bed rubbing my swollen feet. The cool water felt good on my throat and some dribbled down my chin. I lay back down and let myself enjoy Kisa's soothing touch.

"How could I not have my dearest friend at my wedding?" I said. "If there was anybody, besides my mother, whom I wanted to share my happiness with, it was you."

Kisa smiled, but I could feel a tinge of jealousy pass through her fingertips, even after all these years.

"I thought I would burst," I said. "I have never felt so beautiful in all my life. People looked at me as if I was about to join with God himself. Relatives arrived from as far away as Howrah. Massive tents with silk flags were erected all over the grounds. And food...remember the food?" Kisa nodded. "Platters and platters of every fruit known to man. But, best of all...my friends and family."

"It was amazing," Kisa confirmed, still rubbing my feet.

"And then," I exclaimed, "to see that incredibly beautiful man come into sight, to be mine to hold, to adore, to love...it took my breath away." We both sighed. "When he took my hand I thought I would faint from his velvet touch. I could feel his smooth, strong, and tender touch as we walked in a circle around the priest, made our offerings, and said the marriage prayers, vows, and blessings. I felt like tearing off our clothes and taking him right then and there."

We both laughed.

"If I had some magic powder I would have thrown it on the priests and family members and made them disappear." My hand caressed my skin like a soft petal of jasmine as it moved down my stomach and across my thigh. "But, you know how long those stupid priests could drone on and on."

Kisa nodded and smiled. "When Krishnabathi and I were married, our village came to a halt. It seemed like it went on for weeks. I was exhausted...and happy." She stopped rubbing my foot. "You could say I was happily exhausted and not just from the wedding." She raised her eyebrows and we both giggled, then she started rubbing my other foot. "Thank goodness Davidia and I just ran off. It was so much simpler and I don't think any less romantic...well, maybe a little. Staying in a boardinghouse over a dance hall in Benares wasn't quite the same as a palace and feast of gold. But, he's a very giving, caring man, and I have never doubted his commitment to me and the girls."

Something is missing when Kisa speaks about Davidia. I know Davidia loves Kisa, but I've never had the feeling that Kisa has ever loved anyone as much as she did Siddhartha and Krishnabathi. She's accepted a life of security and contentment with someone who loves her. Maybe that's enough. Who am I to say?

"What a night," I agreed, referring to my wedding. Kisa grinned and blushed simultaneously. In all the years we've known one another, I don't believe she's ever heard me speak so intimately about Siddhartha. "I have never felt so complete, so filled, so touched in all my life." My eyes were wet. "He was so tender and yet so strong. His hands, his mouth, his lips—they devoured my very being."

Kisa's eyelids fluttered shut. It seemed as if she was simultaneously imagining Siddhartha's touch. Even though our monthly flows had stopped years ago, I could tell we were sharing the memories of when our flesh was ripe with desire and longed for the men we loved.

"To leave that…to leave me…us…I'll never understand," I said, tears running down my cheeks like a waterfall. Kisa wrapped me in her arms. The earth could have split in two, but we didn't notice. We held on tightly, lost in a flood of memories.

After eternity had come and gone, we wiped our faces on the hand towel Kisa had washed the day before and laughed as hard as we had cried.

"Remember, Kisa, desire is a trap…" I winked, as she finished the sentence, "and desirelessness is liberation." We laughed again.

"Just think," I said. "How many years I believed in that rubbish, only to realize I had done it all out of desire anyway."

"It wasn't all rubbish," Kisa said. "You taught me some valuable life lessons you picked up from Gotama, I mean Siddhartha."

"Name one."

"Well," Kisa thought a moment. "You were an expert at begging. I never saw anybody refuse you food when you held out your bowl." We grinned knowingly, as I batted my eyes and held out my hands with an imaginary bowl. "And," Kisa continued coyly, "You made such an entrance, with the same outfit, again and again." I moved my shoulders back and forth, as if I was walking, showing off a fancy gown.

"Really," Kisa said seriously. "You found some kind of peace and it's rubbed off on me. After all those years of practice and meditation, it was, well, still is, a blessing to be in your presence."

I squinted in disbelief. "Me?"

"Yes," Kisa said. "You are peace and compassion. No matter what's going on around you, no matter how intense the drama or situation, you have always been a calming influence."

"Come on," I whispered. "Stop it."

"Acceptance of praise, however, has not been one of your strong suits," Kisa chided. I blushed.

"Remember when your brother Devadatta came looking for Gotama and said he wanted to 'kill the jackal' for all he'd done to you?" How could I forget?

"You'd only been a nun a short time," Kisa said, "but your compassion preceded you."

"He was hurt," I explained. "He adored Siddhartha. After we were married, he and Siddhartha became good friends. They hunted together. Devadatta looked up to him. He told me how strong Siddhartha was, how far he could shoot his arrows, how smart he was with questions and problems. Siddhartha was more of a big brother to him than a brother-in-law; it's only natural he felt that way." I took a sobering breath. "I had similar feelings. Remember when Siddhartha came home to visit his family and I refused to see him? It had been seven years since he'd left and I still couldn't forgive him."

My heart returned to those difficult days. I remember how embarrassed Siddhartha's father, Suddhodana, had been to see his son in rags, begging for food. At first sight his father refused to see him but was later convinced by his wife, Pajapati, to have an audience with his ascetic son: the son who had studied all the new scriptures, called the Upanishads; who had practiced every form of self-denial known by the great yogis of the time; who had evidently found peace of mind by following his own path and sharing it with others.

Kisa learned about the meeting from Pajapati, who become a stream-enterer (follower) in her later years and traveled with Siddhartha. The king, upon hearing his son's explanations about life, suffering, and liberation, was moved to tears. He wished Siddhartha every blessing and years later, just before his own death, became a lay disciple. Some say he attained the peace beyond all peace, known as samadhi.

Pajapati had said that Siddhartha, at the meeting with his father, had asked about my whereabouts and why I was not in attendance. Pajapati told him that even though I had been in mourning since his departure, I still remained faithful to him as a wife. When I heard that Siddhartha had shaved his head, I did likewise. When I found out that he ate only at certain times, so did I. And when I discovered that he had renounced high beds and fancy clothes, I did the same.

He reportedly asked his disciples, Moggallana and Sariputta, to come with him and warned them that, "the princess is not yet free. She is exceedingly sorrowful. Allow her grief to run its course."

I refused to see him, but the king, my father-in-law, insisted. When Siddhartha entered, I averted my eyes. My anger struck him like a cobra. He said he had caused me unspeakable grief. He said he knew a way for me to release my suffering. Instead of saying he was returning or asking me to go with him, he told me about the Eightfold Path and the Middle Way.

Not once did he ask about our son. I felt I had two confused demons fighting inside me. One wanted to kill Siddhartha, and the other one wished to embrace him.

"I knew what was in Devadatta's heart," I finally said to Kisa. "He didn't want to kill anybody. Those were the only words powerful enough to describe the extent of his pain."

"Whatever you did or said," Kisa added, "turned his heart around like a man and his ox suddenly discovering they were plowing the wrong field."

"I just listened and acknowledged the pain beneath the anger. He wanted the old Siddhartha. He wanted him as he had been, not as he had become. When he realized that things would never be the same, he started questioning all his values and beliefs."

A sharp pain suddenly shot through my chest as if a bull elephant had sat on my lungs. I struggled to breathe and passed out.

Kisa told me later that, "Your face turned as white as marble, then you collapsed like a deer with an arrow in its heart."

Three

When I awoke I heard the fire spark and rain striking the dirt outside. I tried to sit up but was too weak. Somebody in the room stirred.

"Rahula?" I asked. "Are you here?"

"He's on his way," Kisa said. "We sent him word about your health a month ago. I'm sure he's coming. I can't imagine how far it is…Sri Lanka."

"Yes," I replied. "He's coming home. I can feel it. The stars whisper his name. The raindrops send me his prayers. This storm is pushing him, giving him strength."

The thought of my son's return got the blood flowing through my veins, bypassing the clogged areas of my heart. I felt the color return to my cheeks, reached up to Kisa, and cupped her chin. "Thank you, Kisa. Thank you for bringing him home."

"He's not here yet," she said. "And I didn't 'bring him home.' Ananda and I just wrote a letter. We have no way of knowing if he even got our message." Kisa continued, trying to spare me the unneeded pain of false expectations. "And even if he did, there must be a million footsteps between here and there."

"He'll come, Kisa." I took her hand. "He can't let me die without making peace with his father. He can't keep living with such hatred and darkness in his heart."

"I don't know." She looked out at the rain, then back at me. "It's been a long time. Some things get frozen in our hearts and never thaw."

Kisa must have been thinking about her father, his cold-hearted insistence on tradition and the chasm that still remained. She was afraid that she would die before he relented. She'd tried to see him, but he refused. Her mother had pleaded and grown old before her time, trying to intercede on her daughter's behalf.

"Some people never change," she said sadly. "Some keep living but are dead inside."

"Not Rahula," I said assuredly, "and not your father."

Kisa gave a start. "My father? How did you know I was thinking about my…"

"I could see it in your eyes," I interrupted. "He's confused and afraid of the unknown, of all the changes that have been sweeping the land. It won't be long."

"Ha! Not long?!" she retorted. "It's been twelve years. What do you expect, a miracle?"

"No," I said, "compassion."

"Compassion?!" Kisa shouted. "What kind of compassion is it that has a father deny his own child and grandchildren? What kind of compassion is it that keeps a son from seeing his father for over thirty years? Rahula didn't even attend Siddhartha's cremation!" She was livid. "He didn't fulfill his duties, walk around the pyre or crush his father's skull, even though he felt like doing it when his father was alive!"

"It's not a 'kind' of compassion," I replied, after some reflection. "It 'is' compassion. It's beyond transient feelings of hate or love. It's something greater than any one of us or any thing between us. Siddhartha realized it was not a 'thing,' like some have proclaimed. It's not a 'soul' or 'spirit' that lives on and changes bodies. This compassion is something we all swim in, but don't recognize. It's like we're looking at an island, struggling to get there without drowning, and not realizing we are already where we need to go. Our thoughts, desires, and emotions distract us from this truth. They aren't bad, like some yogis and that new Hindu sect believe. We don't need to 'get rid' of feelings or desires. We need to pay attention, to remain awake, to see clearly what is happening and changing within and without, and let go of our judgments about these states, as much as the changes themselves."

"It is in those moments..." I paused and coughed up some phlegm. "It's then, right now, when we are aware, that we can let go of what we see in order to 'be' and experience what we call compassion."

"The only thing I see," replied Kisa, "is my father and your son holding onto the past. I hope they wake up and swim in this sea of compassion you're talking about, but I'm afraid they've already drowned in their stubbornness."

I coughed again. Kisa held out a bowl and put her hand on my back. After the spasm had subsided, she couldn't contain herself and admonished, "I thought you said that Siddhartha didn't 'really' understand compassion at all. I thought you said he had avoided the greatest truth of all."

My head rested on the coarse pillow. "Yes, he did. And that's what hurt so long, until I fully understood." I noticed a wave of emotional pain rise, flutter next to my heart, and subside. "Siddhartha, Gotama, the Buddha, whatever you want to call him—and I'm sure he'll be known by many names—Siddhartha didn't trust the human condition. Because of his experiences in life and his search for meaning, he believed that by paying attention and noticing desire, and thus suffering, when it arose, that one could be free of such attachments and pain. I believe that fully engaging in and enjoying the pleasures of the senses, both good and bad, is the heart of compassion and love."

Kisa looked like she hoped I would stop talking, but, bless her, she just shifted her hips and listened patiently.

"Siddhartha," I said out loud, though I was saying it more to myself than to her, "was afraid of loving someone and experiencing the pain of separation when that person, or he, left or died. He thought it was better to have compassion and understanding for all than to love and be involved with one. He could care about thousands, but couldn't commit to a single individual." My eyes closed. "That's why he left Rahula and me. He was afraid of loving and being loved too much. He was afraid of the pain, the agony...the grief."

I opened my eyes and saw that Kisa was dozing off. As her butt started to slide off the side of the bed, she opened her eyes with a start and saw me smiling. "Oh yes," she said quickly, catching herself. "Yes, I see...afraid of love...couldn't handle it...too scary."

"It's OK," I said. "You don't have to pretend. I have these conversations with myself all the time, whether anyone's around or not. Your presence speaks more love and compassion than thousands of my petty words."

"Oh, no!" she protested. "I've always looked up to you. If it wasn't for you I might still be stuck at home, concealed like a 'good' princess, mourning for Krishnabathi for the rest of my life! You're the one who gave me the courage to look at other men, to realize how short our lives are, and not waste time. You told me to go with Davidia and hold onto happiness whenever I could. I've never regretted it; never. Not even being disowned by my father. If that's the price I've had to pay, so be it."

Memories lined Kisa's face. She was toying with images of Davidia, remembering the day she met him coming out of her father's tent.

She had just been to bathe in the Ganges and was clothed in a wet sari with towels wrapped around her head. Davidia had turned and almost knocked her to the ground. He was in such an excited state that he hadn't been watching where he was going.

Apologizing profusely, he didn't know whether to try to steady her or not touch her at all.

"I am so sorry," he said. "Please forgive my clumsiness. Are you all right?"

She was more than all right. She felt a strange connection and understanding with this man, but didn't known why. "Yes. I'm fine. Please do not concern yourself."

"I apologize again," the gentleman stated. "I have not introduced myself."

"Nor I," she replied.

"My name is Davidia. I am a merchant who has just had the great fortune of obtaining a contract with Bishanara for a monthly supply of silk for his daughter."

"Ah, for his daughter," Kisa grinned. "And would you happen to know the lucky girl's name?"

"Why, no," he replied, as Kisa's servants hid their faces and giggled. "But I am told she is the widow of Krishnabathi and is a beautiful and devoted mother."

"Ah, yes. That she is."

"And what, may I ask, is your given name?" Davidia inquired.

"I must confess," she grinned. "I am Kisa, daughter of Bishanara and the widow of Krishnabathi."

Davidia's face turned red and she thought he would soon cry with embarrassment. "Please, please," she implored. "It was cruel for me to play such a game. Would you be kind enough to join me for tea?"

Regaining his composure, Davidia straightened his clothes, brushed back the wave of black hair covering his eyes, and replied that he would be delighted.

"Are you sure you want to be seen in the company of a widow?" she inquired, with some trepidation.

He replied without hesitation. "I would love to join you for tea. It will be my pleasure." He motioned for her to lead the way. "It's the least I can do for almost running you over."

She remembered feeling his eyes upon her as she led him to the sitting room and was aware of that warm feeling of being admired and loved as a woman. She hadn't felt like that since her husband's death, and she wanted the feeling to continue.

As they entered the dining room, Kisa murmured to her maids to quickly bring some tea, rice, and sweet cakes for her guest. As they ran off to fetch food and drink, one of the maids, Laticima, stopped and whispered to Kisa, asking if this was not a most improper thing to be doing and warning her of its appearance.

"Did I ask you for advice or for tea?" Kisa replied sternly.

"Forgive me, Kisa," Laticima replied, with head bowed. "I am only looking out for your welfare, my lady."

Realizing she'd been rude, Kisa whispered, "Thank you, Laticima, for your concern, but this should be nobody's business but my own."

As Laticima and the others had hurried off to bring the refreshments, Kisa looked down at her wet clothes and said, "Please excuse me, sir. As you can see, I am soaking wet and must go change."

Davidia had indeed noticed every clinging fold of fabric and what lay underneath. He smiled sweetly and said, "Why, of course. I wouldn't want that lovely body of yours to catch cold, would I?"

Kisa blushed with delight and sauntered away as seductively as the circumstance would allow. Once in her chambers she looked frantically for her blue-gold sari with silver lace. "Laticima!" she shouted. "Laticima!"

Laticima came running. "Yes, Kisa. Here I am," she replied, out of breath, having run all the way from supervising the preparations in the kitchen for their unexpected guest.

"Where is my blue-gold sari?" Kisa asked, while putting on another silver necklace, bracelet, ankle ring, and earrings. "I must find it."

Laticima opened one trunk after another until she found the prized possession—a royal blue sari, with hand-painted silver-lined peacocks, orchids, and green lotus designs covering the bottom trim. She hadn't worn it since Krishnabathi had helped loosen its ties on their last evening together, a few weeks before his hunting accident.

Taken aback by Kisa's desire to wear this particular sari, Laticima couldn't restrain herself and once again spoke out as she lifted the garment from its container and protectively carried it to Kisa. "Kisa, this is so special. Are you sure?"

"Yes, yes, I'm sure," she replied, hastily grabbing the brush off her bedside table to untangle the snarls in her wet hair. She stood to let Laticima wrap the sari and placed her hand gently on the maid's shoulder to steady her self. "Laticima, you are like a sister to me and I appreciate your concern and care, but there's something about this man that excites me to no end. I can't explain it. I know it doesn't make any sense, but I must not deny this feeling. It seems like an omen."

"But your father," Laticima interjected, with a furrowed brow, "your father, your mother, they will not understand."

"Perhaps not," Kisa replied, wrapping the last fold around her waist. "But surely, they do not expect me to live the rest of my life as if I were dead, too?"

"I will not say a word, but I can't stop others from talking." Laticima's voice quivered. "You know your parents will find out you've entertained a man in your quarters, without their permission. I fear it will fare ill for you."

Kisa kissed Laticima on the cheek. "My dear Laticima. Thank you for your discretion. I will seek Yasodhara's advice later today. After all," she straightened to comb out the last snarl, "I'm just having tea with the man; you're acting as if we were practicing the Kama Sutra."

It was Laticima's turn to blush. She shook her head. "It's up to you, but remember, if something happens to you it affects us all. It's not just your welfare I'm thinking of."

Kisa returned to find Davidia munching on some sweet cakes with his right hand covered in sticky rice and cinnamon. He gave a start. Licking his fingers quickly and wiping them on his napkin, he arose and bowed.

"I have never seen such beauty in all my life," he said sincerely. "You are like a goddess."

She bowed and sat on her cushion, her knees together and her legs to one side. "Thank you. You are too kind to say such things to this plain girl."

"Plain?" he replied. "On the contrary." He straightened his back and continued. "If I may say so, I travel quite extensively and I have never met one as lovely as you. There is something about you that has touched me deeply." He lowered his eyes. "It is something deeper than your external beauty."

They talked late into the afternoon as if they were old lovers and friends catching up on lost time. He told her about the changes he'd witnessed, how the great cities of Kosambi, Varanasi, Saketa, and Rajagaha were fast becoming new centers of commerce and culture. He described the theater, dancing, and new ideas that were flourishing and taking root. He said that her father, "no offense," was still living in the past; the new man owed his allegiance to his family and friends, not to a local warlord or kingdom. His thoughts rang with truth, yet also frightened her, for they demanded that people choose and be willing to change.

He told her that he had never been married, was the oldest of three brothers, and both his parents had died during the floods. He lived alone in a relatively spacious home, not far from his silk shop in Rajagaha.

"I am not a rich man," he said, before leaving, "but I have more than enough to share."

"Yes, and I have two daughters," she replied. "Surely, you are not interested in a woman in my position?"

"On the contrary," he grinned. "I would be honored to have you as part of my family. I am sure, once you meet, that my brothers and their children will also welcome you into their hearts."

"Well, there is the small fact of my father to consider," she replied, gently brushing her hand against his as they left the dining hall and walked down the path in the garden.

"Your father," he replied. "I'll take care of your father."

"He can be a stubborn old fool," she warned.

"Perhaps, but surely he wishes above all for his daughter's happiness?"

"Yes," she replied meekly. "Surely, but…"

"I'll be back in a month's time," he said. "I will speak to him then."

They walked in silence to the front gate and looked into one another's hearts, understanding their shared destiny.

Kisa was awakened in the morning by the sound of her father's booming voice preceding his entry. His angry words echoed in the hallway.

"In God's name, how on earth could a daughter of mine?! I swear I'll… I'll…" The door burst open.

"Father!" she exclaimed. "I'm not dressed!"

"Don't you 'father' me!" he shouted, striding to her bed and pointing his finger. "How shameful… with a merchant, no less!"

"What?" she replied, already knowing.

"How could you dishonor our name, in my house, without my permission or consent?"

"We only had tea, Father!" Kisa said smartly.

"Only had tea!" her father bellowed. He turned his back and looked out the window. "If you ever, and I mean ever, see that or any man again, under my roof, without my knowledge and a priest present, you will no longer be considered my flesh and blood."

Kisa gasped. "Father, surely you are not serious!" Her tears soaked the covers, knowing that he was.

He turned and walked towards Kisa. He looked like a monster, full of hate, pain, and rage. "Don't ever doubt me," he hissed, then turned and left.

It was then, after hours of crying with her mother Lasha that she had gone sobbing to Yasodhara for advice. Her mother understood but was beholden to tradition and supported her husband's wishes.

Yasodhara, knowing full well the implications of Kisa's decision and understanding the hearts that would be broken, soothed Kisa's tears, held her tightly, and said, "If this man is as he seems, do not look back, do not hesitate, do not deny yourself. Write him. Let him know of your decision."

"But my father?" Kisa cried.

"Your father loves you deeply. His fear and his ignorance may keep you apart, but someday he will realize what he has lost. Someday he will seek the love of the daughter he pushed away."

Not long after those tumultuous days, Yasodhara promised Kisa that she would visit Davidia and see if his intentions towards her were true. She and her mother-in-law, Pajapati, were going to the city in two weeks. It was a trip they had planned for some time, so nothing would seem out of the ordinary. She was also hoping to get a glimpse of Siddhartha, who was reportedly staying on the banks of the Neranjara River in Uruvela, where, it was said, he had converted a thousand Brahmins who had been swayed by his teachings to leave their teachers, the Kassapa brothers, and follow him.

They had heard that Siddhartha was now known as the Tathagata, which means someone whose ego is gone. Or, to put it more clearly, as Jihan, her beloved attendant, had said, "He is no longer attached to his ego. His private thoughts and desires do not hold him captive. That is why they call him the Tathagata."

When the time arrived, Yasodhara bade farewell to her family and, leaving Rahula with Jihan, made her way with Pajapati and several guards and attendants to Rajagaha. It took them a week to arrive. As they traveled Yasodhara informed Pajapati of her intention to visit Davidia. She knew she could trust her with Kisa's secret, but she didn't tell her of her desire to find Siddhartha.

Yasodhara had only been to Rajagaha once as a little girl and did not remember it being so sprawling, noisy, and crowded. A permanent layer of dust hung in the air from all the travelers' carts and animals. She saw some beasts she had never seen before and was told they were called camels, and their owners traveled from the hot western plains.

It took them a day-and-a-half to find Davidia's shop, as they got lost several times in the makeshift tents, huts, and lean-tos along streets that seemed to appear from nowhere and have nowhere to go.

Davidia's shop was large compared to other merchants in the area. The quality and selection of his silks were impressive. After getting lost in blues, reds, yellows, and oranges and picking out several designs for themselves, they asked if they could see the owner.

"Yes, yes, dear friends," Davidia exclaimed, after being summoned from behind several thick curtains. "How can I be of service?"

Yasodhara was the first to speak. Pajapati kept staring unabashedly, as if she was eyeing a prize horse for breeding. "Davidia?"

"Yes." He was surprised. He couldn't remember having met us before.

"We are here on behalf of Kisa," Yasodhara said, without any further introductions.

"What?" Davidia exclaimed, with a smile that shined like the sun. "You have word from Kisa?"

"Yes," Pajapati interjected, snapping out of her appraising mind. "Yes, dear sir. Can we speak privately?"

"By all means," Davidia replied, escorting them to his back office and dismissing his colleagues with a wave of his hand. He offered them a seat and had one of his attendants fetch some tea.

"By what lovely messengers am I granted this visit and news of my beloved Kisa?" he asked, handing them cups of a refreshing cool drink that had black tea leaves floating on top.

"We are family friends," Yasodhara stated, watching him closely. "Her father does not know of our visit. We had planned to visit Rajagaha for some time and, to be honest, wanted to meet you ourselves, for you are all she talks about."

Davidia clearly blushed and momentarily turned away to hide his face.

"My name is Yasodhara and this is my mother-in-law, Pajapati."

Reclaiming his composure he replied, "It is with great pleasure and humility that I..." He hesitated. "Did you say Yasodhara? Are you not the wife of the Tathagata, the Buddha?"

"Yes, I am she," she smiled, "and Pajapati is the wife of Siddhartha's father, Suddhodana. But we are not here for our sake. We wish to know your true intentions towards Kisa."

"My intentions?" Davidia exclaimed. "My intentions are as clear as the day I was born." He moved closer and whispered. "We were meant to be together." They leaned forward to hear his every word. "We could have talked 'till the end of time' and it's until time ends that I wish to have her by my side," he said. "I've never felt like this in my life."

"And you don't mind that she's a widow with children by another man?" Pajapati asked sternly, projecting some semblance of familial protection.

"Kisa asked me the same thing," he said straightening his back. "I told her I didn't care if she had been married a hundred times, had a thousand children, or had been raised as a servant or a saint. In my heart we are already bonded." He sat back and looked at his feet. "That is if she feels the same about me. I know I'm not the best looking, richest, or most intelligent man in the world, but I would give her all that I have and all that I am."

The women glanced at each another with joyful understanding. Kisa had not been mistaken. "We will convey your thoughts to Kisa," Yasodhara stated. "We wish you both the greatest happiness."

"What about her father?" Davidia asked, realizing that nobody had mentioned Kisa's parents.

"We will do what we can," Pajapati replied, "but he is stubborn and set in his ways. If worse comes to worse, you and Kisa must follow your heart and not her family."

As they stood to leave Davidia said, "You have made this the happiest day of my life. I hope you will not be insulted if I tell you that you are both welcome in my home and blessed in my heart."

"The pleasure is ours," Pajapati replied. "You will hear from Kisa soon."

"Yes, Kisa," I said out loud. "Love is a strange companion. It knocks us off our feet, picks us up, and gives us hope for a new tomorrow." I was drifting to sleep, but still mumbled, "Love…I've never…I've never really understood…it's such a…maybe not…"

I heard Kisa say, "Sleep, my sweet friend. Sleep with love."

I dreamed of my visit to find Siddhartha in Uruvela after leaving Rajagaha and our meeting with Davidia.

Pajapati was reluctant to go out of our way, not because she didn't wish to listen to Siddhartha's teachings and learn more about the freedom he claimed to have discovered, but because of the pain and agony she knew it would cause me. But I insisted, and Pajapati had learned long ago that I am not easily swayed once I've made up my mind.

Though the Ordained Followers of the Teacher from Sakya, as they were called by villagers, already numbered in the thousands, it took some time to find them in the vihara (sanctuary) on the outskirts of Uruvela. The vihara had been donated by Siddhartha's devotees Anathapindika and Jeta. The area was called Jetavana and the followers called themselves the Union of Bhikkhus. They were protected in Jetavana, yet seldom remained there long and often slept out in the open.

I was taken aback to see women at the camp, as I had always been under the impression that they were forbidden. Pajapati asked a woman carrying water to a group of men if she was with the Buddha.

"I am a lay disciple," she replied. "We follow our husbands and sons who have been called to live a life of renunciation and seek liberation from desire and suffering." She continued walking and we followed.

"But surely, they have not allowed you to take orders and don robes like the men?" I asked, running to keep up.

"Oh no," she replied. "Being of service to the followers of Gotama is reward enough."

We watched the woman pour her jug of water into the cups of the men with robes and shaved heads. There were not many women present, but one or two I recognized. I saw Yasa's wife and mother, who had left the province, unexpectedly, six months earlier. Rumors that they had gone to follow the Tathagata circulated freely, but I didn't realize they had not only sought the Buddha, but had literally joined their husband and son as lay disciples.

The realization that, unlike most practices of the day, one did not have to leave their family to follow a religious life threw a cold bucket of pain in my face. I stood as frozen as snow on the peak of a Himalayan mountain in winter. Pajapati was hit with the same realization. She saw the shock on my face and realized what I was thinking.

"Yasodhara," she said. "Let's get out of here."

I couldn't move or reply.

"Come on." Pajapati pulled at my sleeve. "Let's go. The carriage is waiting."

I remained immobile. My hands opened and closed stiffly. My fingers turned white and my face crimson red.

"That idiot!" I exclaimed, so loudly that Pajapati tried to hide inside her sari. "What a liar—a thoughtless, selfish liar!"

"Come on!" Pajapati pulled frantically at my sleeve. "Don't make a scene."

"How could he leave us?!" I said loudly, tears sliding down my cheeks. "He didn't have to leave us!"

Pajapati wrapped her arm around me and lead me away as people watched and listened.

"He's a demon!" I cried. "He's destroyed every dream."

"Come, come," Pajapati soothed, her eyes wet with sympathy. "I understand."

"Understand?" I stopped and stared. "How can you understand? He left me; he left Rahula. He discarded us like a sack of rocks. For what?" I motioned towards the followers. "Adoration for a coward—a man who talks about peace, but leaves his family in torment?"

"Stop it!" Pajapati shouted, dragging me into the waiting carriage. "That's my step-son you're talking about, and he's the furthest thing from a demon I've ever known."

Siddhartha had been informed later that day about a disturbance on the outskirts of the gathering. Something about a rich woman yelling obscenities and her mother escorting her out of the area. He wished them peace.

.

four

Rahula had left the island of the Sinhalese, known as Sri Lanka, and was traveling north with his wife Savarna and their ten-year-old son Bodhi. As soon as he had received word from Kisa that his mother was dying, he had notified his employer at the public gardens, Mr. Kannafi, asked his brother-in-law Rama to watch over their home, and packed supplies for the long journey to Rajagaha.

He wasn't a rich man or a beggar. When he'd left home in his late teens, he abandoned his inheritance, his family, and the so-called path to freedom his father professed. He knew Siddhartha was a fraud.

He had found some semblance of peace in a land far removed from his own. He'd learned the customs, arts, and language of the Sinhalese.

It wasn't easy living apart from his family, especially his mother, but he knew he could never face her again without speaking of his father and had avoided doing so for years. Now, with his father dead and his mother dying, he felt compelled to tell her the truth, praying that in so doing it would release the clinging fibers of hatred that were woven through his heart like the threads of a spider.

Savarna understood. She knew the poison her husband kept locked away, the knot in his chest that came between his pure soul and the world. She only hoped that it wasn't too late. She knew it would not be a trip for the faint-hearted and that they may or may not arrive in time, if they arrived at all. Floods, bandits, lack of funds, storms - there were countless obstacles. But she believed in providence, in the power of good over evil, and in the truth that her ancestors would guide and protect them from the land of the northerners, the strangers, the merchants, and thieves.

Their first obstacle was getting to the mainland. Savarna had never set foot off Sri Lanka and taking the ferry across the Gulf of Munnar was never a sure thing. Many had drowned in the crossing on boats that were built from bamboo and over-loaded with every object known to mankind. The more items stowed, the more money the ferrymen made. They had every incentive to add people and goods and none to leave anything behind.

When Savarna stepped on the crowded ferry, placed their few belongings alongside an ox that was straining under the weight of its load, and felt the water washing over her feet, she almost leaped overboard before they even left shore. Rahula was slightly more confident, having come the opposite direction years before and landed safely on the island.

The ferrymen kept urging more and more people on. The waterline kept sinking as the weight increased.

Bodhi thought it was great fun. It was like an animal act, trying to balance a great elephant on a small rolling object. But even though he was ten and everyone said he was becoming a "fine young man," he still held tightly to his mother's long brown vest, which was soaked from the knees down.

Savarna's waist-length black hair was braided and tucked under the hood of her sari. She wore the mark of her religion on her dark brown forehead, between her eyes. It was shaped like an emerald green diamond. She put it on every morning after bathing and before her prayers. She never prayed as fervently as she did that morning on the raft.

About halfway across the straight, her fears came to pass. The ferry started to sway; the waves rose and some of the items on the boat were washed away. It had started out as a sunny day, but the wind had picked up and the ferryman and passengers were paddling as fast as they could, with whatever implement they could find.

Savarna's heartbeat almost stopped when Bodhi was knocked sideways and slid towards the edge. Rahula grabbed him seconds before he would have gone into the sea. None of them knew how to swim.

They eventually landed on the Caramandel coast, freezing from the wind and water, their clothes stiff from the ocean's dried salt. After regaining their land legs and stopping to thank every deity and god they had ever known, they and some other travelers started a bonfire, dried themselves and their belongings, and set up camp for the night. The next morning they headed northeast along the coast, at the bottom of the Eastern Ghats. It would take them at least a week to reach the mouth of the Ganges.

Five exhausting, dusty days later, their journey nearly came to an abrupt end at the Mahanadi River, which widens into the Bay of Bengal.

There was only one ferryman for a hundred miles; his name was Brindhanansi. His arms, legs, and nose were as crooked as his heart. His face wore a permanent sneer and his eyes reflected nothing but greed, deceit, and violence. He was making a killing by charging ten times the asking price to cross the waters. No one knew what happened to the other two ferrymen in the area, but stories circulated that Brindhanansi had driven off one with threats and killed the other man outright. He knew travelers were in a fix and he could ask almost any price, as it took an additional two weeks and necessary provisions to head north to the next crossing.

When they arrived at the Mahanadi River and were told the outrageous price this nasty man demanded, Rahula turned to Savarna in desperation.

"We will return," Savarna said to Brindhanansi and took Rahula and Bodhi behind some mango trees nearby.

"Return?" Rahula inquired. "Return with what?" He pulled the money belt out from under his shirt and showed her what they had for the rest of the journey.

Savarna reached under her vest, inside her sari, and took out a small velvet bag. She untied the string and removed the ruby-studded necklace that had been given for her wedding dowry.

"No!" Rahula shouted. "You can't! It's worth twice as much as he's asking and it's been in your family for generations."

She gently placed her hand along Rahula's jaw. "It's only a thing," she whispered. "It's not you, it's not Bodhi, and it's not your mother."

Rahula hung his head and cried. Bodhi looked towards the river and yelled, "Come! They're leaving!"

They ran to the ferry and, without saying a word, handed Brindhanansi the necklace and walked on. He saw that it was valuable and worth three times the fare he was asking but didn't offer to give them a cent in return. They looked away as he stuffed the necklace inside his filthy shirt and pushed off from the muddy shore.

✐ive

I was staring at the roof as Ananda arrived the next morning. I heard his slight wheeze as he entered and flashed him a smile. I put my shaking finger to my lips and nodded at Kisa who was asleep on a mat next to the bed.

Ananda nodded, quietly placed his basket on the table, and checked my pot for any night soil. He found it empty, returned to the basket, and removed a large papaya. He took a plain, metal-handled knife out from under the basket's cover and slit the fruit down the middle. Walking silently on the balls of his feet to the opposite side of the bed, he reached into the papaya with his fingers and scooped out a bite of golden meat. With utmost care he brought it to my lips.

I sucked the dripping nectar and winked. He laughed.

"So," Kisa exclaimed, rubbing her eyes and stretching, "I see everyone started eating without me."

Ananda's face had turned into a rainbow. He tried tucking his head inside his shoulders, like a turtle, to escape Kisa's gaze. She smiled knowingly, stood, got the pitcher for fresh water, and left for the well.

"Don't be silly," I chided. "Give me some more."

This time it was he that was shaking. I steadied his hand and sucked off more nectar. "This is so great," I said. "Where did you find it?"

"It is from the vihara at Jetavana. Remember how the papaya trees grow so richly alongside the banyan, ebony, and palms?"

"Yes," I recalled. "It is a beautiful place. Are Sariputta and Mogallana staying there?"

"Yes," Ananda sighed as he gave me another bite. "They are aging and can't travel the same distances they used to. But," he sat up, "we have hundreds of newly ordained bhikkhus who are well-practiced in meditation and the precepts and are eager to spread his teachings."

I laid my hand upon his sleeve. "They aren't 'his' teachings, Ananda, remember?"

Ananda frowned. "Of course they're his teachings. Who else gave us the Four Noble Truths and the…"

"No, no, no," I interrupted. "Siddhartha never said they were 'his;' he said he 'discovered them' and found them to be true for his life. We must each find the truth for ourselves."

"Well, of course." Ananda rested his sticky hand alongside the fruit in his lap. "But without his enlightenment and willingness to teach for well over fifty years, we wouldn't have the same opportunity to discover that truth, would we?"

"Maybe, maybe not," I replied. "Who's to say? Perhaps someone else, someone like you, Kisa, or my self, may have had the same insight."

"Don't be ridiculous," Ananda said, dismayed. "Me…Kisa…I don't think so." He looked at me. "You might have arrived at the same understanding as Siddhartha, but…" he looked down, "you wouldn't have been able to teach it. It wouldn't have been allowed. Nobody would have listened."

I looked at my chest, grabbed my breasts, and shook them. "You mean because of these?" I said, then reached down between my legs, "And this?"

Ananda turned away.

"Nobody ever gave us the chance, did they?"

Ananda turned back. "No, they didn't."

"All those ridiculous rules…'A woman bhikkhu can't do this, she can't do that, she has to stay so many feet away from male bhikkhus'…really."

"I've tried," Ananda replied humbly. "It's gotten better."

"Oh, Ananda," I reached for his hand. "You have, and you are doing a wonderful job."

His embarrassment subsided.

"You know, Ambapali is a Buddha," I said, somewhat to myself as much as to Ananda. "If she had been given her full rights and seen in the light of her understanding and devotion to seeking the truth, it is she and not Siddhartha that you and the others would all be talking about."

"Perhaps," Ananda said, "but with her background and all, how could we…"

"You mean because she was a courtesan?"

"Well, to put it bluntly, yes."

I removed my hand. "Oh, I see. An ex-prince is good for the cause, but an ex-courtesan, well—might as well drown her and be done with it."

"I didn't say that!"

Kisa returned with a pitcher of fresh water and caught Ananda's last statement.

"Well, well, well," she said, as she placed the pitcher on the table, "from love to war."

I continued as if Kisa hadn't said a thing, but Ananda turned away, ashamed of his anger, especially in front of Kisa.

"You mean to tell me that out of the thousands of men who have become monks, that not one of them has a thorny or, as you would say, 'sordid' past?" Ananda did not answer. "Look at Kondanna and Yasa! Did they not mate with whores, drink, and gamble in their younger days? And didn't Mukti murder his brother?" Ananda remained silent. "Ambapali did what she had to survive. We aren't given many choices other than wife or whore. Until you talked

Siddhartha into letting us join, we couldn't even lead the same religious life as men."

"I'll see you tonight," Kisa said. She came over and kissed me goodbye and reassuringly touched Ananda's hand. "You two," she shook her head and grinned. "You deserve one another."

As she left I took Ananda's hand in mine. "Ambapali has such compassion. She loves with such a pure heart. Before she learned the Way her body was simply a tool to express that love. Her actions spoke volumes of sutras."

"They sure did," he said to himself, recalling the time he had found Siddhartha and Ambapali late one night behind a grove of Banyan trees. She was kissing his lips and staring into his eyes with accomplished satisfaction. He had tried to turn away but found he could not and remained hidden.

"Remember when she rounded up all those orphans in Kosambi and spent four months finding them each a home?" Ananda nodded. "And that time when Teza and Chevuka were threatening to attack the teachers that had insulted Siddhartha?" He nodded again. "Remember how she spoke to them, as equals, as a sister, and showed them a different way?" Ananda nodded in agreement for the third time. "She has a gift for words."

"She has a gift all right," Ananda said quietly, never realizing the jealously he held towards Ambapali for receiving so much of Siddhartha's time and attention. Ambapali was a sweet, devoted, compassionate woman who, in his eyes, had grasped more of the Buddha's flesh than his wisdom.

"Let's go for a walk," I said, pulling Ananda away from his thoughts.

He hesitated, looked around the room and saw my clothes on a shelf in the corner. Having retrieved them, he placed them on top of the covers.

"Do you need any assistance?" he asked hesitantly as he looked away.

"No, well…actually, yes. Could you hold my sari up while I slip out of this?" I looked at my nightclothes.

He tried to not look, but was unable to fully avert his eyes. I let my nightshirt slip off slowly and took my time wrapping the sari. I couldn't have gone faster, even if I'd tried. For a split second, he looked me straight in the eye.

"Thank you," I said, after tying the scarf around my waist and another over my head. With one arm around my shoulder and his hand steadying my elbow, we walked outside and shuffled down the path past the other shanties, into the filtered light of a cloudy day.

Coming upon a small, well-known local garden that always seemed to appear out of nowhere, we sat on a large, well-worn boulder and admired the Bodhi trees and the lotus flowers floating above the murky water in the center of the garden's pond. The garden had belonged to the Purnapya family and had been gifted to the city upon the elder's death as a sign of appreciation and respect for the community they had made their own for over twenty-five years.

It was a public garden surrounded by crumbling walls of stone that had been carried by cart from a quarry five miles away. Many of the stones had since been taken in the night by newly-arrived immigrants who had no money and were desperate for building materials and shelter.

Nobody touched the inner garden, however, as it had been blessed and dedicated to Krishna, one of the newest deities to gain popularity in a long line of religious traditions.

After a long mutual silence, with birds chirping, chickens cackling, and children playing in the alleyways close by, Ananda said, "Tell me more. How did you live with such pain, for I have never known the depths from which you speak?"

"What?" I whispered. I was in deep meditation and could barely hear his words.

"How did you live with such pain after you and Pajapati returned from your trip to Rajagaha where you had stopped to see Gotama and discovered that other followers had brought along their children and wives?"

I sat with his question for a moment and answered sharply, "I didn't live with it. Part of me died."

Ananda flinched, but didn't falter.

"My illusions, my dreams, my hope for reconciliation and a 'happy royal family' died in a tidal-wave of reality. If I had seen him on that day, at that time, and in that state, I would have strangled him with my bare hands." Ananda blinked at the ferocity of my words. "Pain had burrowed its way deep into my soul, but I don't believe I could ever really injure another being, least of all Siddhartha." I looked down and saw a line of ants heading towards the pond. "In spite of his betrayal, I still loved him."

"Yes," Ananda said softly.

"But I didn't know what to do with that love. I didn't know what to do with such over-powering, one-sided feelings of love. He couldn't take it in. He didn't know how."

"He chose a greater love for all mankind," Ananda surmised.

"No," I said, "it was different, no greater or less."

"What do you mean?"

"We were close in the beginning, but never intimate until our wedding night." I paused, not sure how much Ananda could hear or if he would understand, but I had nothing to lose. "Siddhartha would not allow himself to receive. Do you know what I mean?" Ananda looked puzzled. "He would not enjoy my touch. He always wanted to be giving, to make me happy and provide for my pleasure. He wanted to fulfill my desires, but wouldn't express his own. He was always in control."

Two brown doves cooed their way down to the pond's edge, looked around furtively for danger, then indulged in drink, bending their heads backwards to help the liquid trickle down their throats. A cart passing outside the garden walls startled the pair, who quickly flew up to a safe perch on a nearby roof.

"As long as he was the nurturer, the giver, the lover and not the loved, he was safe. He was a wonderful lover, but his desire to find something beyond desire covered up his fear of being loved in a personal, intimate way. If he allowed himself to receive and accept love, and the care and attachment and dedication such acceptance involves, he would have to accept the fact that the person who loved him could also reject him and leave."

I paused as Ananda filtered facts which must sound like a foreign tongue.

"He was afraid to love Rahula and he was afraid of loving me."

"If that is true, did not his initial fear of loving you become the catalyst for alleviating the suffering of thousands?" he proposed. "Was it fear or awareness of how our pain is caused by holding on to people, illusions, dreams, and beliefs which motivated his departure and desire to teach others the Middle Way?"

"I don't know," I said and smiled. "What do you think?"

"Well," he said thoughtfully, "I never knew him as you have, so I cannot deny or refute your observations or feelings. I can only recall the countless times I saw him reach out to others and help them find understanding and truth in their lives. He didn't do it for fame or fortune, as you know; he had given up those desires years ago. He never mentioned being lonely or regretting his decision to live a wanderer's life, as I have often done." Ananda paused. "He never said an ill word towards another human being, and I believe he truly found enlightenment and peace."

"Of course you do," I said. "How could you believe otherwise?"

Ananda's mouth moved, but no sound came forth. He retreated into silence.

"Oh, come on!" I said, gently pushing his shoulder. "It's just my perception. After I joined the order I never saw him act or speak in a self-serving manner either. His intentions were pure and just." I looked at the pond water as it rippled from a slight breeze. "I'm not sure how aware he was of the roots from which his intentions flowed and how much he used the religious life to avoid sitting still and staying put."

"Sitting still?!" Ananda objected. "I've never seen anyone sit longer in my life!"

"Yes, yes, I know," I said. "I mean living in one place and not moving, staying 'with' someone, as opposed to being surrounded by many. He was as scared of intimacy as you are."

Ananda cleared his throat and raised his hands to object, but I continued. "You followed him for years and denied your own need for human contact. That's why I said, 'How could you believe otherwise?' It's not meant as a rebuke, merely an observation."

Ananda's eyelid began to twitch and his hands shook as the lines on his weathered face deepened. Without warning his arms encircled my waist and his head fell on my bony shoulder. He was crying tears that seemed to flow from a deep well. I was surprised but didn't resist and let his shaking body relieve itself of its long-held grief.

I could almost feel the questions in his head, like insects circling a fire.

"Has it all been a lie?" he sobbed. "Are my days with Gotama and spreading his truth an illusion?"

He lifted his head from my shoulder, wiped his wet cheeks, and gazed into the pond. "What's happening to me? Where did all this doubt come from? Why have you always been the chink in the wheel of my life that's kept me questioning my vocation?"

Without waiting for an answer, he fixed his pleading wet eyes on mine and said, "Marry me."

Compassion prevented me from laughing out loud. "Ananda...my dear friend. I have always loved and respected you and your dedication to Siddhartha and at times can feel his presence through you. I will always hold you close to my heart as a friend and partner in the Way. But marriage…?" I held up my wrinkled hands. "We both know this body I'm carrying will soon lay breathless. No matter how deeply I care for you or another, I will always be the wife of Siddhartha."

Ananda looked away. I put my hand on his face and turned him back around. "I'm not questioning your life or your choices. You and Siddhartha will be remembered through the ages as two of the greatest teachers of all time. There is nothing wrong with the monks life—seeking liberation from suffering and helping others."

My feet started to throb. I looked down and saw that they were swollen but pushed the discomfort away and brought Ananda's presence back into focus.

"Your path is a noble path. I am humbly sharing my experience, my truth, and my understanding."

Ananda's face was drained of color. He was like a fish that had been thrown on dry land. In an unguarded moment he had disregarded forty years of training and offered himself to me, and look what happened? The fear of rejection that had clung to him like his robe had come to pass.

"If I can give up my practice so quickly," he said, "who am I? What's real?"

"You've jumped on the caravan." I said. "You're wandering off with bags of pain and doubt."

"What?" he said, half-aware of my presence, half not.

"I said your emotions have taken you for a ride."

"Well, now that I've finally told you that I love you, you say no. How would you feel?"

My hand covered my mouth in surprise. If anyone knew what it felt like to be rejected or discarded, it surely was I.

"I'm sorry," he said, taking my hand in his. "The tiger of grief took me for a ride."

"I appreciate your honesty," I said, "but you mistake my desire to tell you my story with your need to fix and protect."

The rock upon which we were sitting was growing harder by the minute and the pain in my feet had not subsided. "Marrying me or another will not change our experiences or the truths we have discovered. You will always live with your loneliness, as will I."

Ananda finally noticed my discomfort. "I am tired and cold," he said, looking at the overcast skies. It wasn't that cold. He was trying to spare me the embarrassment of my inability to sit as we had been doing for most of our lives.

"Yes," I pulled the sari around my shoulders. "Let's go back."

As we stiffly rose and stretched, I took Ananda's arm and placed it around my waist. "Thank you," I whispered. "Thank you for your kindness and understanding."

Ananda's pained expression softened. With mutual respect and humility we returned to my temporary dwelling.

Six

Rahula, Savarna, and Bodhi reached Dhaka two weeks after leaving Sri Lanka. They were halfway to Rajagaha and had no way of knowing that unseen forces would threaten their journey and very existence.

Crossing the Mahanadi River had been the first of many tributaries they had to negotiate. As they approached Dhaka and the mouth of the Ganges, they saw wetlands and offshoots of the great river cast before them like large knotted branches that had fallen from the heavens. The branches all lead to the Bay of Bengal where they were challenged by the oceans tides. As they crossed one body of water, another spread its form before them, daring them to swim upon its back or row across its fluid torso.

On the outskirts of Dhaka, wet, cold, and tired, they camped under the stars, falling asleep on the top of a small bluff about a hundred steps from the mighty Ganges. The sky was clear and crisp when their exhausted, heavy eyes closed for the night. They huddled together, blankets wrapped tightly around their shoulders and over their heads. Other travelers and families were close by, a little further down the side of the gentle slope where it was flatter and easier to cook, wash, and lay down comfortably.

Bodhi was the first to awaken when he felt something falling on the blanket. He lifted aside the cover as more drops hit his forehead and saw nothing but blackness. His father and mother awoke but a moment later, looking into the darkness. The thunder erupted seconds before an avalanche of water poured down upon their naked heads. They stood and started to run for cover before remembering that there were no trees in the vicinity and they were blind in the dark.

They covered themselves with the few blankets they had and prayed that the storm would pass, but the storm had other ideas. Instead of passing, it seemed to have set up camp overhead and increased its ferocity.

Their already dampened clothes were soaked through and through. Their flimsy southern garments did little to protect them from the onslaught of driving rain. If the storm didn't wash them away, they were sure they would freeze to death.

Savarna, always the shy, traditional wife back home, had been transformed. She was the one who'd dealt with the crooked ferryman; she'd been the one who suggested traveling with others to ward off thieves; she had publicly manifested the strength Rahula had always privately relied upon and admired. It was Savarna who reassured Rahula and Bodhi. "The Gods wouldn't have let us make it this far to be washed away and forgotten."

As she spoke they heard the roar of the river edging closer to their precarious bluff. Screams escaped from those camped below, then silence, as the waters edged higher and higher. Bodhi trembled and Savarna felt his fear. For some reason she couldn't explain, she was calm. She held her son as Rahula held her.

"Hello!" A muffled voice rose through the den of darkness. "Hello! Is anybody there?"

They strained to see where the sound was coming from and saw a lantern through the sheets of rain. "Over here!" Rahula shouted. "Over here!"

As light came closer, they saw the shape of a man and a small raft as it almost ran them over but was stopped by the few inches of land that remained.

"Hurry!" the man shouted. They jumped onto the floating vessel. "Here. Sit down here, in the middle, to keep balance."

This was no time to hesitate or ask questions. They did as the man said. Rahula realized they must be floating over the very spot upon which they stood moments before.

The man rowed towards the water's edge. They could hear his labored grunts and groans as he fought against the rushing river. Rahula made no attempt to help, certain he would capsize the small vessel if he made the slightest movement.

Lights appeared in the near distance. "Here, Rampal! Over here!" could be heard between the thunderclaps. "Yes…this way!" They hit shore with a jolt, or what remained of the shore.

"This way!" said the man who had shouted the boatman's name. He helped them step off the raft. "Moksa!" their savior shouted to the man on shore. "Take them quickly. They're freezing!" Rahula, Savarna, and Bodhi felt a large tarp or covering being wrapped around them as they were led away.

The glow of the lantern revealed a path leading uphill. They saw more lights ahead and heard people shouting. "You crazy fool!" one man said. "You could have drowned!" admonished another.

Moksa and Rampal didn't reply. They walked silently with the shivering family they had rescued. They lived in the small farming community of Shedradan which, fortunately for Rahula and his family's sake, was located on a steep ridge above the merciless Ganges.

"Here," Moksa said, as they were taken inside a dwelling. He handed Rahula, Savarna, and Bodhi some clothes and dry towels. "Get out of those wet clothes and put these on." They did as they were told and moved next to the hot fire to change. Moksa turned away as the shivering family stripped, dried off, and got dressed. When they had finished he turned and said, "Sit." They sat on a thick carpet, staying close to the burning wood. Moksa put dry blankets over their shoulders and handed them each a cup of steaming tea. "Be careful there, son. Don't burn your tongue."

As their shaking subsided and the warmth of their blood returned, they took notice of their surroundings. The hut was rather large, made of clay and straw, and had no windows. The only opening, besides the entrance, was a small vent in the roof where the smoke departed and a gap in a wall through which Rampal appeared.

Moksa went to Rampal and hugged him tightly. "Don't ever do that again!" he said, as he stepped back and hit him in the shoulder with his fist. He turned, went to a corner, grabbed some clothes, and returned to face Rampal, who was rubbing his shoulder and smiling. "Put these on, you big fool," he demanded. Rampal walked in front of the fire, stripped off his clothes without shame (as Savarna looked the other way), put on the dry garments Moksa had provided, and sat with an exhausted thud.

"How did you find us?" Rahula asked.

"I remembered seeing a bunch of you folks settled down on the banks when I came home from the fields," Rampal replied, as Moksa handed him a cup of tea and sat down with his own.

"I told him not to go," Moksa interjected. "We didn't think anybody was still alive, but he insisted."

"He would have gone himself," Rampal stated, "if he knew how to swim." They grinned knowingly.

"We can never repay you," Rahula said.

"Ah!" exclaimed Moksa, "they speak!" He smiled broadly, revealing a gap where his two front teeth were missing. He had dark curly hair that was clean and shiny and a broad plump face with pointed ears and dimpled cheeks.

"There is no need," replied Rampal, who was a large man with big hands, broad shoulders, and graying beard. "You would have done the same for us, I am sure."

"Words cannot express our gratitude," Savarna whispered. "You not only saved our lives but have made it possible for us to get to Rahula's mother before she dies."

"What?" Rampal replied gruffly. "My Sinhalese isn't that good. Slow down."

"She said," Rahula explained, "that you saved us for a reason. She believes it is destiny."

"I am Savarna," she continued. "This is my son Bodhi and my husband Rahula. Rahula's mother, Yasodhara, is failing. She is the wife of Gotama, known as the Buddha, the Tathagata. Have you heard of her?"

"No," Rampal replied, stroking his beard. "Can't say that I have, but I've heard of this Buddha fellow."

"His people, what did they call themselves?" Moksa pondered. "Bhikkias, Bhakes, Bhikkhus...something like that. Anyway, they came this way a couple years ago on their way to Dhaka. They talked about this and that and mentioned their teacher's name."

"Seemed like a nice bunch of folks," Rampal recollected.

"Well," Savarna said, "she's doing badly and we have to pay our respects before it's too late."

Rahula frowned at Savarna, not wanting her to speak about their personal lives.

"What?" she exclaimed, correctly interpreting his expression. "They just saved our lives," she whispered. "Don't you think they deserve to know something about us?" Rahula didn't argue. He smiled politely and bit his tongue. "Bodhi and I have never met her." Bodhi's head rested in her lap. He was asleep. "He's never met his own grandmother," she said sadly.

"Well," Moksa said, as he rose to get more tea. "I hope she's as nice as you expect."

Rampal leaned forward and, referring to Moksa, quietly said, "His grandmother won't have anything to do with him...says he's no grandson of hers."

"I'm sure it will pass," Savarna said.

"It's been twenty years," Rampal replied.

"That's cruel," exclaimed Savarna, shocked that anyone would say such a thing to their grandson. "What happened?"

Rampal slowly took a sip of tea and said, "Don't really know. Maybe because of us, maybe not."

"Because of 'us'?" Rahula said.

"Yeah," replied Rampal, looking into the fire. "You know, us living together and all."

"What's wrong with two friends living together?" Rahula asked in dismay.

"Good question," Rampal replied. "Why don't you go ask his grandmother?"

"Well," Savarna said hopefully, "I'm sure my mother-in-law is different. It's been said she's lived like a saint."

Rahula put his arm around her. "I don't know if she's a saint, but surely she will love you as much as I."

Savarna kissed Rahula, thanking him for his reassurance. Rampal looked up at Moksa, who walked towards him with more tea, and grinned from ear to ear.

"We got the right people," he said, as Moksa sat down beside him.

"What?" Moksa replied.

"I said it was worth it," Rampal surmised, having witnessed the love and affection between the young couple before him.

"What was worth it?" Moksa wondered.

"Finding them," Rampal repeated.

"Why do you say that?" Moksa replied, looking quizzically at Rampal. "Of course it was worth it."

"I'll tell you later," Rampal whispered, smiling lovingly at his housemate.

Seven

"Here!" Chitra exclaimed, hurrying over to Devadatta and handing him a covered bowl of freshly made curry. "Don't forget to take this."

He lifted the silk covering, smelled the spicy aroma, and said, "If I don't eat it first."

Chitra smiled. "No, you don't!"

Devadatta grinned back, both knowing it was one of his rare attempts at making a joke. Chitra played along as he pretended to lift the cover and start drinking.

"If you don't leave that alone I'll make you stay and look after the grandkids all day," she threatened, referring to their daughter's twin girls, Desai and Jamashee, who had recently turned three.

With a look of mock horror Devadatta quickly put the cover over the bowl and lowered it with both hands. "Oh no!" he exclaimed, putting the bowl on a nearby table and running after his granddaughters, whom he proceeded to pick up under each arm and spin around. "Not that! Not these dreaded little imps!"

The girls' surprise quickly changed into gleeful screams and shouts. "Fast, Papa-ji!" squealed Desai, as Jamashee giggled incessantly.

After a few more turns Devadatta put the girls down, held his hand to his forehead, and said, "I better stop before I fall down. The room is spinning." His granddaughters pulled at his white cotton robe and yelled between laughing and falling down. "More, Papa-ji! More!"

He leaned down and kissed them both. "Later, my sweets; I've got to go see your Auntie Yasodhara."

"More!" Desai shouted, trying to follow. She tumbled sideways and sprawled onto her back.

"Now look what you've done!" Chitra rolled her eyes, as the girls followed their grandfather, pleading for him to pick them up again. "Come on," Chitra said. "Let's go out in the garden and play peek-a-boo with the sun." She took both of their hands and led them towards the back door. "Give Yasodhara my love," she said, turning her head towards Devadatta. "I'll see her tomorrow."

Devadatta nodded and walked out the front door. As he strode down the street towards the opposite side of town, carefully holding the bowl of curry, his sliver of joy with his granddaughters slipped away as he thought about his sister. Not one to reveal emotions in public, let alone in private, he kept his locked deep behind his daunting exterior of privilege as a high caste Brahmin and prince from Sakkya.

People bowed their heads, put palms together, and moved to the side when he approached. He seldom returned their greeting. His thoughts deepened as he walked past the herb shop, Davidia's house of silks, the candle maker, and several food stalls. The street was streaming with foot traffic, carts, vendors, bhikkhus, beggars, gamblers, yogis, children, and endless crowds moving with no apparent direction or purpose.

As he walked past the open sewers, which ran into the river, he thought about his life as a young man and how much he had taken his sister for granted before she had been betrayed. He had watched her drowning in sorrow and his nephew Rahula growing up without a father. It was then, when he, too, had been wounded by his good friend and brother-in-law, that he knew how much he loved his sister.

He had trusted Siddhartha with his deepest thoughts and fears. He had told him about how distant he felt from his own father, about being scared to stand up to him or tell him what he thought. He told Siddhartha about his first sexual experience with a woman in the village and how ashamed he had been for not knowing what to do.

Siddhartha listened. He always listened. He told Devadatta to not worry about what others thought or said. He taught him to be true to himself, to live a virtuous life of good deeds, and to provide for his family. Siddhartha had accepted him as if he was his own brother. Then, in spite of all his fancy words, the man he trusted left like a thief—no farewell and no explanation, free of all responsibilities.

After Siddhartha vanished, Devadatta spent more time with his sister. At first it was their grief and hatred for Siddhartha that tied them together, but later, as Yasodhara's hatred and shame subsided and they saw each other age, he began to appreciate and care for her as an equal. He realized that they shared the same history and childhood. He began to love her as a sister and as a friend.

Two kids in rags rushed past, almost knocking the curry out of his hands and distracting him from his thoughts. "Hey! Watch where you're going, you little hoodlums!" They paid him no attention and ran off into the crowd. "No respect," he muttered. "Kids have no respect for their elders anymore." He cleaned some curry that dripped from the side of the bowl and held the cover more tightly. "The whole world's going to pieces."

Yasodhara and he were close, but he knew there was more to her than met the eye. There was something different about her, something he had never seen in another, not even his wife. It was something akin to grace or enlightenment, though he hated to use that word, enlightenment. It had such baggage and the lies…you couldn't trust anybody who said they knew what it was. They didn't have a clue.

No, Yasodhara had found something better. It was hard to define. He couldn't talk about it, but he could feel it when he was with her. She made him feel complete, happy, like he mattered. Some would call it compassion. Others called her a saint. He just knew her as his sister, as family, and he'd never met anyone kinder or more forgiving. She was everything he wasn't, and he longed to be like her.

Eight

We returned from our walk and entered the hut. Ananda brushed off the dust that had accumulated on my backside and clung to my sari like honey. His lifted his hand and stopped when he neared my bottom.

"Stop it," I said, "a little dust won't kill me." I sat on the edge of the bed. "Would you bring me some water?" I nodded at the pitcher on table. Ananda was pouring us both a cup when there was a thudding knock on the entrance frame. Devadatta ducked under the archway, then straightened to his full stately height.

"This place is a dump," he said, without a hello or how are you. "You can't be serious about staying here?"

"Devadatta," Ananda said, after he and I had shared a quick smile over Devadatta's abruptness. His lack of tact could be wonderfully refreshing one minute and exceedingly annoying the next. "Welcome. We just returned." He held me by the shoulder and lifted my legs onto the bed.

"Just returned?" Devadatta exclaimed. "Returned from where?"

"We went for a little walk down to the garden," I said, a little short of breath, as Ananda placed some pillows behind me and pulled the thin cover over my lap.

"What?" Devadatta bellowed. "You're supposed to stay in bed! Remember what the doctor said?" He turned towards Ananda. "And you're supposed to be her friend!"

Ananda looked down and smiled, bemused, knowing this was how Devadatta expressed his concern.

"Leave him alone, you big bag of wind," I blurted. "I asked him…no, I insisted that he take me out. Don't blame him." I coughed and sat up. "If you want to yell at someone," I coughed again, "yell at me." I couldn't stop coughing. Both men came to my side, concern etched across Devadatta's stern features.

"Here," Ananda offered, "drink." He handed me the cup of water and I drank slowly. The coughing subsided.

"I have to escape this room every now and then," I told him, patting the bed for him to sit down by my side. "Twenty-four hours a day in this palace, even for me, is a little much."

Devadatta sat down stiffly, aware of Ananda's watchful presence. He kept his distance, not used to someone outside the family being so intimate with his sister.

Ananda understood Devadatta's reluctance. "I'll be back tomorrow," he said, nodding in my direction, understanding my brother's need for privacy.

Devadatta barely acknowledged Ananda's departure and didn't hesitate to barrage me with his concerns. "What will it take to get you out of this dump?" he questioned, looking around the small hut with unguarded disdain and revulsion. "Chitra and I have asked you…" he hesitated, "no, we've begged you to come live with us." He sat tense and rigid as a tree and kept himself just out of my reach. "You could be living like a queen. We'll hire somebody to care for you. You don't have to depend on Kisa and your so-called friends." He nodded towards the entryway, referring sarcastically to my just departed Ananda.

I coughed again and leaned forward. Devadatta put his hand on my back, looked around for the cup of water, and practically ran to the table to retrieve it. "Here," he said. I coughed some more, drank a sip or two, and felt Devadatta's gentle hands help me lay down.

"My sweet brother," I said softly, "is it you or I who am living in this body?" He looked away. "Is this your home or mine?" He didn't answer. "What would you do," I took his hand in mine, "if you were sick and I came to your home and insisted that you come live with me?"

"That's different!" he turned back. "I have the means to care for myself and a wife who..." He stopped himself, remembering my dead husband. "I'm sorry. I mean, I have people around and all the money I need. You have nothing and, I dare say," he looked around the hut, "no one here."

"I have all that I need," I said smiling. "I am richer than you will ever know." Devadatta looked bewildered, like he had just had a huge bureaucratic mess of unsolvable problems thrown at his feet.

"Please, don't start," he said. "You know I don't believe in that spiritual gift stuff."

"That's not what I mean. I really do have everything. More food than I can eat, plenty of water, and Ananda and Kisa watching over me."

"But they're not family," he said. "It's not the same. Chitra and I..."

"You and Chitra are very dear," I interrupted. "I appreciate all you do and all you've ever done, but Kisa and Ananda know me well. We've been through light and dark together. While you were here in Rajagaha, Ananda and I were traveling, teaching, and sleeping under the stars up and down the Ganges. We've known each other for over forty years." I looked directly at my dear brother. "In some respects, he knows me better than any man alive."

There was nothing he could say so he sat in silence, head bowed, and heart, as usual, slowly softening.

"And Rahula is coming," I said.

"Rahula?" he exclaimed. "Coming here?"

I nodded.

"How do you know this?" he asked with wide-open eyes.

"Kisa and Ananda wrote him a letter."

"Sent where?"

"Sri Lanka," I said. "They wrote several weeks ago."

Devadatta was shocked into silence. He hadn't seen his nephew for decades.

Rahula was like a son to him. He had always gone to Devadatta for advice; for comfort he went to Yasodhara.

At his fourth birthday party he asked his uncle where his father was. Barely able to hide his rage, Devadatta ignored the question.

"How would you like to go visit your grandfather?" he asked instead.

"Oh yes!" Rahula shouted. But on the way to his father-in-law's compound, Rahula asked him again, "Where is my father?"

He squatted down, eye-to-eye with Rahula, put his hands on his shoulders, and said, "It is best to not speak of your father, understand?"

Rahula didn't understand, of course, and asked, "Why?"

"Just don't," he insisted, "especially in front of your grandfather, OK?" Rahula nodded obediently. "You promise?" he asked for assurance. Rahula nodded again, tears in the corners of his little body's eyes.

Rahula kept his promise and never asked his uncle or grandfather about his father. He did, however, talk to his mother about it, and at seven years of age he met his father for the first time.

When it was learned that Siddhartha planned to visit, he spoke to Yasodhara about revenge. After days of intense discussions and heated arguments, he promised to not lay a hand on him. He avoided the entire affair. His heart had ached for Rahula, sensing the mixture of love and revulsion they shared for Siddhartha.

He hadn't been surprised when Rahula, in his teens, had fled. It broke his heart and Yasodhara's, but he understood his nephew's need to distance himself from his famous father.

"Now, now," Devadatta said protectively. "Just because they wrote him doesn't mean he can come."

"He'll be here before the monsoons."

He shook his head. "Anything can happen."

I touched Devadatta's cheek. "Don't worry. I know what I know."

He was holding everything in. He wanted nothing more in the world than to see Rahula, but he didn't want his hopes dashed like a ship on a rocky shore.

*N*ine

Rahula, Savarna, and Bodhi bid farewell to Rampal and Moksa the next morning and headed north along the Ganges, their baskets full of fresh fruit and bread supplied by their newfound friends, who refused any kind of payment. They had given them directions and suggested areas to stay and places to avoid along the way.

Bodhi was coughing roughly from the drenching the night before. Savarna didn't say anything, but she was alarmed. She knew that traveling in the cold open air might exacerbate his condition.

"Here," she said, bundling him from head to toe with a blanket. "Keep this on."

"Mom!" Bodhi complained. "I don't need it. I'm not cold." He started taking it off.

"Keep it on," she insisted and put it back over his shoulders. "I don't want you getting sick."

"Mom!" he exclaimed, sulking like a two-year-old. He walked ahead so she couldn't reach him, then pushed the blanket halfway off his shoulders—just enough to claim his independence while not disobeying her altogether.

"Leave him alone," Rahula said. "He's fine."

"I don't think so," Savarna replied, "and I don't want to take any chances, do you?"

Rahula looked at his half-covered son. "Of course not," he replied, walking up next to Bodhi, taking the two ends of the blanket hanging off of Bodhi's back and tying them together under his son's neck.

"Dad!" Bodhi sneered.

"We need to take care of ourselves," he said, taking another blanket he was carrying and wrapping it around his own body. When Bodhi saw his father wrap up, he didn't struggle as much with his own.

"Besides," Rahula said, nodding back at Savarna, who was about to catch up, "it doesn't hurt to give your mother a little peace of mind, does it?"

Bodhi grinned, in spite of himself.

"It doesn't what?" Savarna asked, as she came along side.

"It doesn't hurt to be careful," Rahula said.

"No, it doesn't," Savarna smiled, "nor to be prudent and wise."

Rahula and Bodhi glanced at each other and Rahula rolled his eyes and laughed. Savarna picked up the pace and walked ahead, the bottom of her blue sari blowing left and right from the chilly north wind that danced down the Gangetic Plain.

That night they camped as far away from the Ganges as possible, without getting too far off-course, and bedded down in the foothills of the Vindhya Mountain Range. They were making good time up the valley that spread underneath the Himalayas like a large thick blanket. As they covered up for the evening, next to the fire they had built from scraps of wood and twigs found on the slopes, Rahula said, "If we keep this up, we should be there in a couple of weeks."

Bodhi tried covering his mouth to muffle his cough, but it was louder when they stopped moving. Savarna was alarmed but glad they were making such good time.

"I hope we can keep it up," she replied. "As long as his cough doesn't get any worse, I think we'll be OK."

"He's a strong boy," Rahula said proudly. "He'll be fine."

Savarna kissed Rahula's lips. "Yes, he is. He takes after his father—strong and kind."

Rahula beamed. "You give me the strength," he whispered lovingly. "You give us both strength."

Bodhi's coughing subsided, for the time being. Within minutes his sleepy breath deepened and Savarna felt his tired body against her back. She was snuggled up behind Rahula, sandwiched between husband and son. Nothing on earth felt safer or more content then to be together under a star-filled sky with those she loved. Her arm encircled Rahula's trunk, her hand on his chest, his back and hips against her breasts and stomach.

She watched the fire over Rahula's shoulder as the last embers burned and listened to the sounds of the night. Small animals skittered through the underbrush. Rustlings, rumblings, and unfamiliar sounds of creatures, streams, and shifting rocks kept her vigilant, as she felt Rahula's chest rise and fall. His quiet snoring joined the symphony of the unseen.

Rolling onto her back, she stared up at the stars and thought about their honeymoon—the first night she and Rahula had ever slept together. It was in her father's house in the country. Actually, outside her father's house.

"Let's sleep in the open air, under the stars," Rahula had suggested. "It's too cramped and confining in here." He glanced at the walls of the small vacation home her father kept in the highlands.

She agreed, wanting to do likewise, but not daring to say anything that might be contrary to her husband's wishes. She had been taught by her mother and grandmother to always be of service, to be subservient to her husband, and do as he commanded. Though Rahula had never been one to insist on anything, let alone that she act as his maid, now that they were officially and spiritually married she wasn't sure what to expect.

They pulled some bed linens out to a clearing. The air was warm and the moon was full. She wasn't sure what to do next. She had never undressed in front of a man. Rahula, likewise, had never been with a woman.

"Would you like me to get undressed?" she finally asked.

"If it pleases you to do so," he replied.

She watched him watch her and felt their mutual excitement and apprehension. As she removed her last garment and stood naked before him he exclaimed, "You are more beautiful than I ever imagined." Though she couldn't tell in the moonlight, she was sure she blushed from her toenails to the crown of her head.

When he began to take off his clothes she started to turn away, but a deep desire took over and she couldn't avert her eyes. They stood facing one another with tender innocence, desire flashing between them like bolts of lightening in the night sky. She felt like she was being sucked into a heavenly fire. One minute they were standing naked in the moonlight; the next thing she knew they were covering one another with kisses, their hands exploring every crevice, every inch of the other's existence.

It wasn't long until she felt the pain of his entering and the tearing of the covering that had protected her womb from conception. Not realizing she had screamed, Rahula stopped and asked if she was OK, if he had hurt her. She replied, "Please don't stop. I'm fine." Her mother had warned her about the pain and explained that it would only last a few minutes. She was right. It was on that night, or one of the many that followed, that Bodhi was conceived.

Savarna was only seventeen on the day of her marriage, but on that night she felt ageless, as if she had discovered the greatest secret in the universe.

All the training she had received from the women in her life, about how she should behave with her husband, became irrelevant with Rahula. In public he made the decisions, but in private he said that was rubbish; they were equal partners. He only went along with the customs to not ruffle feathers or upset her parents. "After all," he had said, "I didn't come here to start a revolution; I came to avoid one."

They had their arguments, but they never lasted long. The one subject that had always been closed for discussion was Rahula's father. Whenever she mentioned Siddhartha, Rahula walked away. "Whatever happened?" she wondered.

She knew that the teachings of the Buddha, the Gotama of Sakya, were spreading in Sri Lanka, as well as its political influence. Years before Rahula had appeared, a man called Ananda ventured to their island and enticed many to follow the path of the man who had awakened, the Buddha. Some of her uncles and nephews joined this group, which caused bitter divisions between the elders and believers of other faiths. She came to understand that this teacher, the "Awakened One" as he was often called, was Rahula's father.

When followers of the Buddha learned of his death, there was great lamentation and rituals of mourning. When Savarna heard of the Buddha's passing, from her nephew Janarapadha at the market, she rushed home to give Rahula the news. Upon hearing of his father's death, Rahula stood perfectly still, closed his eyes, flexed his hands into fists several times, and sighed. Opening his eyes, he proceeded to get dressed and left for work without so much as a kiss or word of farewell. He didn't say anything about it when he returned home that night, nor had he since.

Savarna's eyes slowly closed. Bodhi coughed several times. She rolled onto her side, put her arm around Rahula, and slept in short spurts, awakening frequently to Bodhi's congested cough or the eyes of unknown creatures staring back at her in the dark.

Ten

Ambapali was in secluded meditation at the vihara of Jetavana. She was bald, having cut off her silky black hair when she joined the Sangha. She wore a simple brown robe with a single sash tied at the waist. In her early seventies, her arthritic knees were acting up far more often then she liked to admit. She had to sit on a small stool or recline completely to meditate for long periods of time. Her once sensuous hands—hands that had caressed and brought hundreds of men pleasure in her younger years—were now knotted and swollen like her knees. The skin around her eyes was lined with wrinkles, but her cheeks and lips retained the soft, alluring quality she had had when she first gazed upon her future mentor and lover, Siddhartha. It was in those dark brown pools of her now enlightened eyes that the Buddha, Siddhartha of Gotama, had temporarily strayed, allowing his senses to define his consciousness.

It was one of Ambapali's nuns, who brought her one bowl of food per day, who told her of Yasodhara's failing health. Without explanation or hesitation, she picked up her shoulder bag and begging bowl and informed the other nuns, who were also on retreat, that she was going south to see her in Rajagaha.

"But she's not even a follower!" Bishaka, one of her younger disciples, exclaimed. "What about us, your devotees? We need you here."

Ambapali put her hand gently on Bishaka's shoulder. "Yasodhara is my friend. There is nothing greater than the love of friends."

"But she no longer follows the Way or practices the precepts."

Ambapali smiled. "She lives the Way. She is as much a Buddha as you or I." She bowed to Bishaka, turned, and walked away, leaving her devoted devotee staring at her backside, pondering how an old woman who had left the order a decade ago could be compared to her beloved, enlightened Ambapali.

As Ambapali left the protected encampment, a torrent of emotions, thoughts, and images assaulted her memory. With relentless ferocity they took her into the past, provoking anxiety and doubt about seeing her friend, the woman whose husband she had laid with, consuming his body and his mind for years on end.

Shortly after Siddhartha's death, she tried to bridge the unspoken gap of misunderstanding between Yasodhara and herself, but Yasodhara told her there was no need to talk of the past. "We both loved the same man," Yasodhara proclaimed, tears streaming down her face. "There is nothing wrong with love."

"No," she insisted. "I loved what he stood for, what he had become."

"I loved him as a man and as a teacher," Yasodhara replied. "He was my first love and my last."

They embraced as sisters.

Her expression of sympathy and attempt to take down the fence that had been erected between them while they lived together as nuns were heartfelt. They finally acknowledged that the fence existed and agreed to open the gate to forgiveness.

She knew that she and Siddhartha had been seen together several times. When she first joined the order she had taken every opportunity to seduce him, to find out what he was made off. For some time she had been successful. Even though they were painfully discreet, she had felt the eyes of others in the night, the eyes of those who would not and could not understand her need to discover if this was the Buddha, the Enlightened One, or simply a man with human needs like all the rest.

She stumbled on a root and stopped from falling by grabbing onto a knotted branch that looked like her hands. As she found her balance and told herself to pay more attention to what was in front of her, an image of her mother, who had also been a courtesan, came upon her.

Her mother was thirty and she was fifteen when she realized what her mother did to survive. She had promised that she would never follow in her footsteps. Her mother promised to find her a respectable husband to marry. How she could fulfill that promise was a mystery, but one her mother had tenaciously held to her death.

They had been walking along a path, like the one she was on now, when her mother stopped dead in her tracks and fell to the ground convulsing, phlegm oozing from the corner of her mouth. She remembered screaming, "Mother! Mother!"

Her mother's eyes rolled back in her head as her jaw clamped shut. Her breath came in spurts. She shook her again and again crying, "Please! Somebody!" But no one could hear her cries. It was soon over.

It had been quick, without warning. She leapt from her mother's side and ran. She ran and ran, as fast as she could. She ran to her uncle Sikhura's house and told him what had happened. In spite of his wife's lamentations to not get involved with "that woman," he followed Ambapali back to his sister's body and brought her home for cremation and religious services.

After the funeral Sikhura offered to take in Ambapali, but his wife would have no part in it. "I won't let a woman like that in my house!" she insisted.

"She's just a kid," Sikhura replied. "She needs a home."

"She's old enough to know what to do with you," she'd said venomously.

"Don't be ridiculous," he said. "Where's she supposed to go?"

"She can stay with her mother's people," his wife spat. "They'll take care of her."

"Take care of her?" Sikhura surmised. "You know what they'll do."

"It's where she belongs," his wife concluded. "I won't allow a whore in this house!"

Ambapali overheard their conversation. She was ashamed and left in the middle of the night. Not knowing where else to turn, she found her way back to her previous residence, the House of Yoniatma.

After several lonesome months of mourning, she was "put to use" and "taught a trade." She began her training in the art of Kama Sutra, the art of making love, and was taught how to minister to and please men.

"I'm sorry, Mother," she said out loud, as she walked towards Rajagaha, being careful not to stumble again and fall on her face. "I did what I had to do."

She had been very successful at her vocation. It gave her access to many powerful and wealthy men but never brought her happiness or peace. She soon realized why her mother had wanted her to take a different path.

It wasn't until she encountered Siddhartha in her mango grove that she ever entertained the thought that there was something more, something beyond the known, the physical. His words sparked a smoldering fire that lit her curiosity. She became determined to see if his words were real or more false promises. She vowed to find the truth, even if it cost her some clients or, ironically, sullied her reputation.

Five years after following the Buddha's teachings and meditation practices from the time she opened her eyes in the morning until she fell asleep in the night, Ambapali discovered that she knew so little and wanted to experience everything. She left her courtesan life, took her vows to follow the precepts, and lived as a nun.

There was a particularly long winter when the brothers and sisters of the Sangha (believers of the Buddha's teachings) had been in retreat throughout the rainy season. Ambapali finished eating her only meal of the day and was mindfully washing out her bowl, contemplating its emptiness, when she awakened to something beyond herself, something that was greater than her ego or self-consciousness. It was indescribable, yet she tried.

"It felt like a rush of air filling a gigantic void inside my heart," she told Pajapati and Yasodhara. "It is as though 'I' do not exist, yet here I am. Everywhere I look I see one heart, one love." They listened rapturously, trying to absorb some of the peace and wisdom she radiated. "It's not something I can hold on to. If I try to contain it, it blows through my fingers like the wind. If I try to grasp it or label it, it melts like dew drops in the sun." She looked fervently into their eyes. "I wish I could give you this joy, this happiness and peace."

"Oh, but you have," Yasodhara said. "We can feel it."

"You're like a warm fire," Pajapati smiled. "We are basking in the glow of your compassion."

Thirty-eight years later the glow remained. She had become so unselfconscious that she was often not aware of herself as a separate entity. As long as she was in her physical body, thoughts, emotions and sensations would continue, but her compassionate nature was so ingrained that people wanted to be around her, to touch her, to bask in her presence.

Now, if her knees would allow it and the rest of her aging body permit, she would see Yasodhara once again—the woman who had shared her intimacies, fears, and joys, the one she had unintentionally hurt beyond comprehension.

"Hold on, sister," she whispered between labored breaths as she walked towards Rajagaha. "Hold on, sister of my heart."

Eleven

Ananda was the one who had sent word to Ambapali about Yasodhara's illness. He'd waited a number of weeks before doing so, not sure if it was the right thing to do, but after the conversation at the Purnapya Garden and his embarrassing proclamations of love, he was certain that Ambapali had a right to know. He knew that Ambapali and Yasodhara could live with the truth of their history much better than he could himself.

Ananda saw his life tediously unfolding before him—never finding the ultimate prize, but continuing to teach up and down the Ganges, meditating, walking, sitting, eating, faithfully following his teacher's footsteps, spreading the word about the Four Noble Truths and the Eightfold Path of right views, right aspirations, right speech, right behavior, right livelihood, right effort, right thoughts, and right contemplation.

"I've done everything 'right' for so long," he muttered, as he dumped cold water from the nearby stream over his head for his morning bath. "Where is my bliss, my happiness? Where is the joy of samadhi, of freedom from suffering and desire?" The water made him shiver. "I must become like a novice," he reasoned, putting the empty bucket on the ground as he watched a group of newly ordained bhikkhus walking towards him.

"I can recite the Four Noble Truths in my sleep and could proclaim them from the ashes of my funeral pyre. I know suffering exists and its cause," he ruminated, walking a few steps and sitting down on his worn blanket, waiting for his audience with the newcomers. "I know the remedy to suffering is the cessation of attachment, but I can't let go of Yasodhara."

The monks arrived, bowed, and sat before him.

"Namasté," he said.

"Namasté," they replied.

"A thousand blessings…may all beings be happy, free from suffering, and at peace."

"Thank you, Master. And you." They bowed again.

"What questions have you brought today, my young seekers, samanas of the Tathagata?"

Brother Jotikkha spoke first. "How does one remain faithful and follow the way without any understanding or inner validation for what one seeks?"

"Blessed is he who asks the question," Ananda said out of habit, wondering if this student was a devil in disguise. How did he dive into Ananda's head and grab a hold of the very demon he was wrestling with?

"The Blessed One said to be 'full of faith, anxious to learn, and modest in heart,'" Ananda stated. "Faith is a gift of hope." He coughed and pulled his robe tighter. "When traveling we are given directions or a map and believe them to be true, correct?" They nodded. "Yet, we do not know what we will encounter along the way or what awaits us at the end of the journey. If we keep our attention focused on the map, we will reach our destination."

"What if we follow the map and are being led in circles?" Jotikkha asked.

"Have faith," replied Ananda, not sure if he believed the words escaping from his lips. "Trust what you believe and hope for in spite of your momentary experience."

"But," Jotikkha continued, "when do I know I've walked far enough and long enough to turn around and ask for a new map?"

Ananda recalled asking Siddhartha the same question in Pava, where they had their last meal together.

"When you keep bumping into the same tree," Siddhartha replied.

"What?" Ananda asked, dismayed at his teacher's response.

"It's not a matter of taking the right map or walking far enough," Siddhartha smiled. "It's watching where you're going."

The Buddha finished the last bites of rice his body could digest and continued. "When I first began my search, I tried everything. Each thing I tried led partway, but none of them took me home. It wasn't until I walked my own road, without a map, and watched where I was going that I arrived."

Ananda listened with every fiber of his being. "Tathagata," he questioned, "I've paid attention, listened, practiced, and taught, but I'm still not sure where I'm going or if I'll ever find what you have obtained."

Siddhartha gazed compassionately upon Ananda and said softly, "Ananda, some times it takes many lifetimes to break the cycle of birth and death. Do not despair."

"I don't know if I can wait another lifetime," he replied sadly. "This one has been long enough."

Siddhartha smiled patiently.

"Master...Master?"

Ananda heard someone calling and saw Jottika and the other disciples sitting before him.

"Yes," he replied, regaining the present. He straightened up and lifted his head. "Yes. What is your question?"

The monks were concerned. Jottika repeated the question for his teacher's sake.

"I said, when do you know you have walked far enough and long enough before you turn around and ask someone else for a different map?"

"Yes," Ananda replied, "a question of faith." He paused. The novices waited. "I believe...I think..." he trailed off, then said, "I don't know." Another long pause ensued. "That is something we must discover for ourselves," he finally stated. "I can't tell you when enough is enough. I don't know when it's been enough for me, let alone for you."

"But, if you don't know," Jottika exclaimed, "who in the world does?"

Ananda laughed. "Look within. Stop trying to 'get somewhere' and pay attention. That's what the Buddha instructed. He said, 'Don't despair. Your time will come.'" He left out the possibility of it taking "many lifetimes."

The disciples looked uncomfortable and hesitated to ask more questions until Jhana, a handsome young bhikkhu with a beatific face, said, "What do I do with desire? How do I navigate desire's muddy waters and float on its surface, like the lily pad?"

"You don't," Ananda exclaimed, surprising himself. "You just jump into the muck, keep swimming, and hope you catch a breath of fresh air and insight every now and then. It's impossible to 'stay above' desire and suffering. It is at the core of our being and surrounds us like air."

The astonished monks didn't know what to say. They weren't sure they heard him correctly. When they realized he was not speaking in a parable, Jhana said, "But the Buddha surely didn't teach us to swim in desire?"

The Buddha had sunk in enough desire for the lot of them, Ananda thought. He had enjoyed the fruits of his young wife Yasodhara and later been taken into the arms of Ambapali, while he, on the other hand, had lived a celibate life of devotion. He could have been with a woman, perhaps even Yasodhara, if only he had been the Prince of the Sakyas.

"Why can't she accept my love?" he wondered. "She's still a little sixteen-year-old holding on to her dead husband. Even now, in her last days, she pushes me away."

The old monk pondered his life while the devotees waited impatiently. Suddenly, as if shot from a cross-bow; Ananda remembered Jhana's question—the question that had sent him reeling through the land of remorse and regret.

"No. He didn't tell us to frolic in the muck and get what we can," he finally replied. "We all get our feet stuck in the mud. It will happen hundreds of times, no matter how diligent we are in our attempts to avoid it."

"Look," he said, shaking his finger at the disciples. "Siddhartha wasn't a god. He was flesh and bones just like you and me." He looked into their faces. "He made some mistakes and he didn't have all the answers."

He rested his hands in his lap. "Let me tell you a story. The Tathagata said, 'Every thing is transient. Nothing lasts forever. There is death, birth, decay, and growth; there is coming together and separation.' Sometimes we come together and other times we're torn apart. It doesn't always feel good or seem fair, but that's how the world works. Siddhartha, I mean the Buddha, said, 'The restless nature of the world is the root of pain. Self is but a combination of composite qualities and its world is empty like a fantasy.'

"I loved a woman," Ananda told his shocked audience. "I loved her with all my heart, but it only brought pain because

she didn't love me in return. I thought I had been crushed."
He thought about his proposal in the garden. "It happened
when I was a young man and again, not so long ago. But, I'm
still here. I'm still breathing, climbing up the stem, out of the
darkness, and onto that lotus flower in the sun.

"Suffering happens, but we do not have to cause more
suffering. We can choose to be honorable and respect others."
He closed his eyes. "We can begin again, living mindfully
with honesty, love, and compassion."

Twelve

Chitra had waved farewell to her granddaughters a few moments before Devadatta returned, when their daughter stopped to pick them up on her way home. She loved spending the day with Desai and Jamashee, but also found it exhausting.

"I don't have the energy I used to," she told her husband. "Another day like that and those two would have been the death of me." She gave Devadatta a welcome home kiss.

"How is Yasodhara?" she asked expectantly.

"Not good," he replied, brushing the dust from his jacket.

"Let me get you some tea," Chitra said, hurrying to the kitchen, calling the maid, and returning to take her husband's jacket. "You must be tired. It's quite a walk to that side of town."

Devadatta sat on the teak wood chair in the living room as Chitra rubbed his shoulders. "Did she like the curry?"

"Oh, I'm sorry," he replied, looking around the room. "I forgot to bring the bowl back."

"No worry," she said. "Did she like it?"

"I don't know. She didn't try it. She'd been out walking," he said. "Can you believe it…walking? I get her the best doctor in town. He tells her to stay off of her feet, but as usual she never listens."

"If she was up for it, what's the harm?" Chitra replied.

"What's the harm?" he shouted. Chitra took her hands

away and stepped back as Devadatta turned. "He said if she
didn't rest it could kill her. That's what the harm is."

"I'm sorry," Chitra said quietly, as the maid brought in
the tea, setting it on the table and quickly retreating to listen
from the other room.

"That Ananda character," Devadatta continued. "I don't
know what she sees in him."

"They've been friends a long time." Chitra pulled a chair
over and sat beside him. "He's been a tremendous help. I
hear he visits every day and brings her food and water."

"What's wrong with us?" he demanded. "Aren't we good
enough? My God, we're family and she refuses to stay here!"

"It's her choice," Chitra replied. "She's not your little
sister anymore. She's a grown woman and has the right to be
where she chooses."

"Yeah," he replied quietly, "a grown woman—an old
grown woman."

How did she end up like this, he wondered, born into
wealth and privilege and dying in a rat hole? He thought of
happier days.

"Faster! Faster!" she shouted. He was giving
Yasodhara a piggyback ride. He was ten. She was
eight. It was a hot day and they had gone to the
highlands with their parents to cool down.

"Come on! Are you a tiger or a sloth?" she egged.

His ten-year-old legs were going as fast as they
could. He wasn't that much bigger than her at the time
and was getting winded, but he had to prove that he
was as strong as his cousin Siddhartha, who was
carrying their cousin, Anuruddha, on his back
towards the finish line.

"Go, Siddhartha. Go!" Anuruddha hollered.
"They're catching up."

They were almost neck-and-neck when Siddhartha, who was bigger and stronger, put on a burst of speed and glided well ahead to the finish between the banyan trees.

They all fell to the ground, laughing and chiding one another on a race well done. All except him, of course. He hated to lose. "You cheated," he exclaimed, pointing at Anuruddha and speaking to Siddhartha. "He's not as big as Yasodhara. You didn't have to carry so much weight."

"Cheated?" Anuruddha yelled back. "I weigh just as much as your little sister and you know it!"

"You do not!" she yelled. "You're a lot smaller. He's right; we should have had a head start."

"No way!" Anuruddha pushed on Devadatta's shoulder. "You're just a sore loser!"

"Am not!" He pushed back.

"You're right," Siddhartha said quietly.

"What?" Anuruddha turned with surprise.

"He's right," Siddhartha repeated. "Let's call it a draw."

Devadatta puffed out his chest. "See. I told you so."

He remembered seeing Yasodhara give Siddhartha a quick smile of thanks for making the peace.

Devadatta took a drink of tea, set his cup on the table, and stared into the swirling liquid. "She'll always be my little sister," he said. Chitra put her hand on his hairy forearm. He looked at her, then back at his tea. "She said Rahula is coming."

"What?" Chitra exclaimed. She looked towards the kitchen and waved for the maid, who she knew was listening, to go fetch her a cup of tea.

"I said Rahula may be heading this way."

"Oh my!" she exclaimed. "That would be wonderful. Praise the gods."

"We aren't sure," he said. "It's a month's ride from here, at least. For all we know he never even got the letter, and if he did...he could be lost or..."

"He made it there, he can make it back," Chitra assured.

"There is no guarantee," he said. "You can't trust Southerners, let alone the weather."

"He'll make it," Chitra replied. "If he's anything like his favorite uncle, he'll make it in record time."

Devadatta let a grin escape, made sure the maid wasn't watching, and kissed his wife's cheek. "Let's hope you're right."

Thirteen

"Run! Run!" shouted Rahula, as he picked Bodhi up under his arms and headed towards an impression in the hill. Savarna was close behind. He turned and yelled at Savarna again. "Hurry; they're getting closer!"

She hitched up her sari and ran alongside her husband and son. The sound was like thunder. Their feet slid and bounced on the ground as it heaved. They plastered themselves against the shallow crevice just as the stampeding elephants ran by, their eyes wild with fright.

They had avoided bandits by following Rampal and Moksa's advice. They had traveled in numbers and kept to the center of the plains. Now, just as they were about to traverse their last major obstacle, the Aravalli Mountains, some idiot had tried to catch a baby elephant. His attempt had angered the herd. People scattered to safety, but Rahula and his family had found themselves caught in the gigantic mammals' path with nowhere to turn.

As the last tusked male lumbered by, blowing his trunk, Bodhi coughed violently from the wave of dust. It was so thick they could barely see one another.

"Bodhi." Savarna covered his mouth and eyes with her sleeve, hoping that would alleviate the irritation. His coughing continued and they tried to comfort him, to no avail. His cough had worsened over the last several days and this was not helping. It was deepening and dangerously persistent.

"What happened?" Rahula exclaimed, after the last elephant had passed.

"We're lucky," Savarna reasoned, as her breath returned. "I didn't think we would make it, did you?"

"I wasn't sure," Rahula panted, gasping for air.

They all rubbed their eyes, blinking to wash away the dust and dirt.

"We've got to find him a doctor," Savarna insisted. "It's getting worse."

"Yes, I know," Rahula agreed. "Let's go back to Kanpur."

"That's a two-day journey," Savarna exclaimed. "We can't wait that long."

"I doubt if there's an herbalist in the village we passed this morning," Rahula reasoned, "but we can try."

Carrying his coughing son on his back, Rahula and Savarna backtracked and asked everyone they met if they knew of a healer in the vicinity. Late in the afternoon they came upon a woman washing clothes at the river. Her children were close by. They expected her to reply like all the others, that there was no help in the area.

"Yes," she said, as she rung out a shirt on the rocks and yelled at one of her kids to stay away from the river's edge. "Let me finish and I'll take you to her."

Rahula and Savarna shared a hopeful glance.

"Here," Savarna said, "let me help." She got down on her hands and knees, took a wet sari out of the basket and pushed, twisted, and shook it in the wind, then folded it neatly and placed it on top of the other clean clothes in the adjoining basket. The women smiled and they quickly completed their task.

"I am Henna," the woman said, as she picked up her basket and called to her children. "Come. I will take you to my mother." She looked at Bodhi, who was clinging to his father's back and coughing. "She can cure anything." They followed Henna towards the small village.

"Your mother?" Rahula asked.

"Yes," Henna replied, "my mother."

"I am Rahula and this is Savarna," Rahula said. "This bag of rice on my back is our son Bodhi."

Henna stopped short, as one of her youngest bumped into the back of her legs. "Did you say 'Bodhi,' like the tree?"

"Yes," replied Rahula, "like the tree, strong and wise."

"The Bodhi tree is the same one under which our Lord Buddha awoke to his true nature." Henna said.

"Yes," Rahula said sharply, then saw the admonishing look from Savarna. "Yes, so we discovered."

"Are you followers of the Tathagata?" Henna inquired, as she lifted the basket onto her head.

"No," Savarna answered, before Rahula said something to offend their guide. "But we have heard of his great deeds and compassionate heart." Rahula looked away as Savarna came alongside Henna. "Are you a follower of the Tathagata?"

"Yes," she smiled. "We became disciples after hearing him speak. I was just a little girl, but my mother remembers him well."

They walked the rest of the way in silence. Rahula wanted to find a remedy for Bodhi's cough but hated the fact that it might come from a disciple of his father.

They reached the hut as the sun set. Henna told the children to put away the clothes and start a fire for dinner. She went inside to look for her mother, then returned.

"She's not here," she said. "Mother! Mother!" she yelled.

"I'm out back!"

Henna took her guests into the backyard where they saw an older woman sitting on a blanket. She was separating greenish-red leaves from their yellow stems.

"Mother," Henna said, "this is Rahula and Savarna. Their boy..."

Bodhi coughed, as if on cue.

"Yes, yes," her mother said. "I understand."

She stood and went to Bodhi. Her fingers were stained red. "How long has he had the cough?" she asked, placing one hand on Bodhi's back while feeling his pulse with the other.

"About eleven days," Rahula said.

"Eleven days?" Henna's mother exclaimed. "You're lucky the boy's alive."

She looked in Bodhi's eyes and put her hand on his chest. "What's your name, son?" she asked.

"Bodhi," he said weakly.

"Bodhi? That's a strong, holy name," she grinned, exposing her yellow teeth.

"Thank you, Ma," Bodhi whispered.

"Ah," she chuckled, "and so polite!"

Henna whispered to Savarna and nodded at her mother. "She's called Ananda Ma. I've seen her perform magic. If there's a way to heal your son, she will."

"Blessings on you and your mother," Savarna said.

"Bring him inside, out of the evening air," Ananda Ma instructed Rahula, who followed her into the hut.

Once inside she had him lay Bodhi on a cot. The children had started the fire and were boiling some rice. They stared into the flame and stole glances at Bodhi. Savarna counted seven in all.

"Where is their father?" Savarna asked Henna, as they dished out the rice.

"He's dead," she replied matter-of-factly.

"I'm sorry," Savarna said.

"We get by," Henna replied.

"How did he...I hope I'm not prying."

"No," Henna answered, as she lovingly bopped one of the kids on the head. "Pick that up." The child, who must have been three or four, picked up the branch she had dropped and placed it on the fire.

Savarna handed Henna a bowl. "He died from malaria." She looked into her bowl, then up at Savarna. "Our youngest two joined him."

Savarna was speechless. The thought of losing a child was unbearable. Though she'd seen it often enough back home, it gave her the chills.

"My mother was ashamed that she could help so many, but not her own family," Henna explained. "She refused to speak or use her knowledge for months. The brothers of the Sangha eventually convinced her to not add bad karma by letting others die needlessly."

"And you?" Savarna asked. "How have you survived?"

"I didn't think we'd make it," Henna said, "but the bhikkhus brought us food and taught the oldest children how to read and write. They spread the news about Mother's ability to heal and sent pilgrims and followers to us for help. From the food, wood, and money we've received for Mother's gift, we have never gone hungry."

"But," Savarna said, "how did you survive in here?" She placed her hand over her heart.

Henna stopped eating. "I had never known such suffering, but I had to carry on." She looked at her children as they ate, took another bite, and said, "I give thanks every day for what I have."

Savarna ate quietly and said, "We have nothing to give you."

"You owe us nothing," Henna assured.

"Where did your mother go?" Rahula asked, as he sat by Bodhi.

"She's outside making a concoction for your son," Henna replied. "She'll eat later."

Henna gathered the empty bowls and shooed the children outside for one last romp before bed. Savarna helped wash the dishes, making sure to leave one covered bowl of rice for Ananda Ma.

"Why are you traveling so far from home?" Henna asked.

"We are going to see Rahula's mother in Rajagaha. We received word that her end is near."

"You're welcome to sleep here. You can curl up on the ground by your son. It's crowded, but you'll be warm." She smiled and handed Savarna a dry bowl.

They had all bedded down for the night when Ananda Ma entered quietly, stepped over all the sleeping children, and made her way to Bodhi. He had covered his mouth to muffle his cough and not wake the others, to no avail.

"Here," Ma told Bodhi. "Drink this." She handed him the cup and helped him sit up. Savarna, who couldn't sleep, arose and watched. She and Rahula had laid next to Bodhi.

Ma turned to Savarna and held up a bowl of pungent liquid. "Have him drink this three times tonight. He won't like it."

Bodhi gagged on the cupful he had just swallowed and almost heaved. His facial contortions could scare away the worst demons, but he kept it down.

"Blessings to you and your family," Savarna whispered to Ma.

"Let us pray for the Buddha's blessings," Ma replied. "These herbs are strong and should dry up the moisture that has been captured in your son's chest, but without the help of Buddha and the Bodhisattvas, it is nothing."

"Thank you," Savarna said, wanting to believe. "We saved you some rice. It's on the table." She pointed it out in the dimming firelight.

Ma bowed deeply, as if it was she who had just been given the gift of life.

"Lie down, my sweet." Savarna laid Bodhi back down. "Get some sleep."

It wasn't long before she felt him drifting off, only his cough staying awake. She went over to the table where Ma was eating and sat beside her. Little light remained from the fire's embers. Rahula felt Savarna leave his side and lay awake listening to his wife and Henna's mother whispering in the dark.

"Henna said you heard the Buddha speak," Savarna questioned. "Is that true?"

"Yes," Ma replied. "I had the good fortune to hear the Blessed One speak the Dharma."

"What is the Dharma?"

"Dharma," Ma explained, "means truth."

"The truth about what?"

"The truth about life, freedom, and the end of suffering."

"How does one find this end to suffering?"

"By realizing that everything is impermanent, that everything changes." Ma slowly inhaled and exhaled, remained silent for a moment, and continued. "Every breath comes and goes. Nothing remains."

"What remains?" Savarna asked. "What is permanent and everlasting?"

"Ah," Ma sighed, "that is what you must investigate. That is what the Blessed One discovered and compassionately shared with all."

"Isn't there a soul, a spirit, a god that cares for us?"

"No." Ma said bluntly.

Savarna was shocked. She had been taught since childhood that some gods were kind and creative and others wrathful and destructive. Her parents and her parents' parents made offerings, prayers, and sacrifices to these gods for everything in life. Without the guidance of the gods, everything was turmoil. Nothing would make sense. She had never considered otherwise.

"Then...then what is there?" Savarna asked.

Silence.

"If there is no soul or Atman that continues after death, what is there?" Savarna asked again.

Bodhi coughed. Several children talked in their sleep. Henna was laying awake in the middle of her children, listening.

"Awareness," Ma eventually replied. "Awareness."

"Awareness of what?"

"Everything that comes into consciousness and everything that falls away."

"I don't understand."

"Watch your breath," Ma instructed.

Savarna tried.

"Each breath rises and falls, comes and goes."

Savarna felt her chest expand and contract.

"Who is it that's breathing?" Ma asked.

"Me," Savarna replied. "I am."

"Who is 'me' and 'I'?" Ma inquired.

"Me...Savarna...wife of Rahula, mother of Bodhi."

"Those are labels," Ma corrected. "Who is it that's watching your breath? What forms consciousness?"

"I don't understand," Savarna said sadly, wanting desperately to understand her dead father-in-laws teachings.

"Maybe this will help," Ma said. "The Buddha told us a story about a man who was born blind and did not believe in the world of appearances and light. Because he couldn't see the sun, the moon, or the stars he denied their existence. He told his friends, who insisted that they did indeed exist, that they were all deluded and were seeing illusions. He said if colors existed he should be able to touch them and feel them.

"There was a well-known physician who was called upon to see the man. The physician mixed four elements and applied them to the cataracts, which had caused his blindness. Upon doing so the man obtained his sight and realized that his belief in what was real and not real no longer applied.

"The Blessed One is like the physician, the cataracts are the illusion that there is a separate self or soul, and the four compounds applied to the blind man's eyes are the Four Noble Truths."

After a long silence Savarna said, "Thank you for your patience, but I still don't understand how we can live without God. Our lives would be pointless."

"It's not pointless. Everything matters—every action and every word. Deeds echo through the valleys long after they've been acted upon."

"If that is true," Savarna concluded, "your good deeds will be echoing for centuries."

Later that night, after Savarna had given Bodhi his third dose of medicine, she felt Rahula sitting by her side.

"It's lessened," she said. "It doesn't seem as deep."

"Yes," he replied, "I can tell."

"Thank God for Ananda Ma," Savarna whispered, "or should I say the Buddha?"

Rahula cleared his throat.

"Sorry," Savarna said quickly. "That's what she believes. She doesn't know he's your father."

She reached out in the darkness and felt Rahula's face.

"Yes," he replied, "I heard."

"What do you think?" she asked quietly.

"What do I think?" Rahula said, a little too loudly for Savarna's comfort. "I think it's the same rubbish I heard all my life."

"Well," she said cautiously, "whether you believe her or not, they do a lot of good. Surely their karma will increase."

"Yes," Rahula agreed, "that I cannot deny."

They stayed with Henna's family another day and night, continuing to give Bodhi the herbs, amazed as his strength returned and his cough subsided. But they had to carry on and venture north.

As they departed, Savarna bowed on her knees to Ma and Henna. They lifted her from her prostration, embraced, and cried together.

Rahula and Bodhi approached and bowed respectively. "There is no way we can ever repay you," Rahula stated. "You have given our son his very life."

Some dust drifted up Bodhi's nose and he sneezed. They all laughed.

"We are the ones who are blessed by your visit," Ananda Ma beamed. "We will never forget you."

As they turned to depart Ma added, "There is no greater blessing I could have received then to minister to the grandson of my blessed Lord Buddha."

Rahula whirled around, looked accusingly at Savarna, who shook her head, indicating she hadn't said a word. He confronted Ma. "How did you find out?"

"I don't sleep much at night and my hearing is excellent," she replied with a wink and a grin.

"Please don't tell anyone," he implored.

"It will be our secret," Ma assured, putting her hand on his heart. "Go in peace."

They all put their hands together and bowed their final farewells.

"May your mother be free from suffering," Henna said as Rahula, Savarna, and Bodhi waved.

Several of Henna's children followed the Buddha's grandson until they were out of sight, heading towards the last range of mountains that stood between them and Yasodhara.

Fourteen

As Rahula and his family were making their way over the Aravalli Mountains, referred to by the locals as the Baby Himalayas, Kisa was winding her way through Rajagaha to spend the night with Yasodhara. Before leaving home, she had a frustrating encounter with Davidia.

"I understand," he said, "that Yasodhara needs someone, but does it have to be you every night?"

"Who else is there?" she said sharply. "Ananda can't be there night and day. He's got thousands of monks depending on him."

"Why don't you get her sister-in-law to stay or, better yet, why don't you tell her to move in with her brother? They can give her everything she needs."

"You don't understand," Kisa replied. "She wants her last days to be with those she knows and trusts."

"I think you're the one who wants it this way," Davidia said, taking his wife's hands in his.

Kisa looked away, then turned back. Tears dripped onto their joined hands. "I have to be there. She's my best friend."

"I understand," he said, pulling her closer. "Just don't forget about me, OK?" Kisa nodded against his shoulder. "I miss you," he whispered.

"I know," she said.

"Give her my love," he said, placing his hand gently between her breasts, "and take mine with you."

She smiled but didn't reply; she couldn't return the sentiment. Respect, yes; admiration, yes; security and gratitude, yes. But passion, fulfillment…the kind of love she had known with Krishnabathi?

"How did I get so lucky?" she questioned, walking through the streets. The city was quieting down and people hurried home through the twilight. "Two men who love me, both in one lifetime," she mused. "I don't deserve such good fortune. Well," she corrected herself, "maybe I do. Yasodhara always says we get what we ask for."

She wished her father would accept her as his daughter. Her mother wrote and said she was coming to see her and the children and had added, "Your father remains as stubborn as ever."

"That old fool," she thought as she quickened her step, not wanting to be caught out in the dark.

"You don't have to come every night," I said, upon Kisa's arrival. "I'm fine by myself."

"Yeah, sure," Kisa replied, "and I'm the Queen of Champa." She checked my night pail, saw that it was empty, and looked at the cup of water sitting on the stand. "You don't need me?" she admonished. "Then how do you explain this?" She held up the cup.

"I'm not thirsty."

"Even if you were," Kisa retorted, "you can't drink this. It's filthy."

She threw the dirty water outside, refilled the cup, and came back in. She held me up in bed and said, "You've got to drink." I took some sips and coughed. "I don't want you shriveling up like a dried leaf," she chided.

After the coughing subsided she helped me into my clean nightgown, lay on top of the covers, and told me about her mother's plan to visit.

"I would like to see your mother. It's been a long time since I had the pleasure of her company. Remember when your mother was visiting with Visakha?" Kisa nodded. "Visakha lived in Savatthi and gave the bhikkhus her Eastern Garden."

"She had so much money," Kisa exclaimed. "I think she's even richer than my mother."

"Yes, and a ton of children and grandchildren. I could never keep track of who was who." We shared a grin. "Your mother was there when Visakha invited Siddhartha and those with him to her house to dine. We were all privileged to accompany him to her 'summer home' for the evening.

"We had just sat down when Visakha asked Siddhartha, 'Lord Buddha, I humbly ask that you grant me eight favors.' Not knowing what she was talking about, he said he wouldn't consider her request until he knew what they were. She said, 'I saw that the bhikkhus' robes were tattered from the rain. I would like to supply robes for the Sangha every rainy season for the rest of my life.'

"You should have seen your mother's mouth drop open. The thought of spending that much money on a bunch of wandering monks horrified her. Before Siddhartha could say a word, Visakha continued, 'I would also like to provide food for those coming and going from the garden, food and medicine for the sick and provisions for those who care for them, bathing robes for the bhikkhunis (the sisters), and rice-milk for your followers year round.'

"By then your mother had almost fainted from shock. Visakha had just promised more than your father and mother have given their entire lives.

"'Why are you offering such comforts and charity?' Siddhartha asked.

"'My maids and I saw how tired your bhikkhus were after traveling such long distances, then having to beg for food,' she explained, 'and they have no garments in the rainy season and are cold and wet with nothing to change in to.'

Everyone strained to hear her explanation, especially your mother.

"'Lord,' Visakha continued, 'when your followers are sick, if they do not get proper nourishment or medicine they will get worse and possibly die.' Siddhartha was smiling like a baby by then.

"'Furthermore,' Visakha said, 'I wish to provide rice-milk for all the bhikkhus because it will help them be of clear mind and body, as you have said several times.'

"'What advantage does this give you, Visakha?' Siddhartha questioned.

"'Oh Blessed One,' she concluded, 'is it not to my advantage that the bhikkhus be healthy, so they may attain nirvana and spread compassion and goodness to all, helping free the world of suffering and confusion? Is it not to my advantage to have a community of like-minded individuals striving to live the truth, thus supporting my personal practice? Is it not, dear Lord, to my advantage to increase my good karma by helping the Sangha?'"

Kisa and I were acting like little girls staying up late, whispering under the covers. "By then your mother had recovered and was listening. It looked like a storm was brewing inside of her, as if she had been tossed on an unknown island and was searching the horizon for a way home."

"So!" Kisa exclaimed, "That's what caused it."

"Caused what?" I said.

"Caused my mother, as my father said, 'to go spiritual on us,'" Kisa explained. "He meant being charitable. For a few months after that dinner party, Mom started giving to the poor and went out of her way to provide bhikkhus with food and clothes. Father said he had to watch her like a falcon or we'd soon be living on the streets like beggars."

We cracked up. Kisa tried to regain her composure as I continued.

"After Visakha had explained why she wished to provide for the bhikkhus, Siddhartha closed his eyes. When he opened them he was far, far away. Without looking at Visakha he said, 'Noble woman, disciple of the Tathagata, thou givest from a pure heart. You spread joy and relieve pain. Your gift will be a blessing for others as well as yourself.'"

I rolled onto my back. "I've never seen someone so ecstatic about giving away their money. Upon hearing Siddhartha except her request, Visakha was so bloated with joy you could have popped her with a pin."

"Did anyone ever argue with Siddhartha? You know, question his sayings or want the Sangha to go in a different direction?"

"Good Lord, yes!" I said.

I coughed and tried to clear my throat. "A little water, please. I feel parched." Kisa took my cup, went to the pitcher, and re-filled it to the brim.

As she returned she tripped on the end of her sari, which was partially undone and dragging on the floor. She leaned forward, spun around like a top, and fell hard on her bottom. The water flew into the fire, almost extinguishing the light, as the cup hit the wall and cracked down the middle.

She was dazed, like a newborn deer that had fallen, not sure how to make its legs work. I sat up, stared at my friend sprawled on the floor with her sari twisted around her legs like knotted yarn, and tried not to laugh. Kisa looked up, then at herself, and squealed with laughter. We laughed so hard I thought I might pee in the bed.

"It's a good thing my kids can't see me now. They'd never let me live this down."

"Don't think that I will either."

After some further maneuvering, Kisa untangled and rewrapped her now dirty sari and got me another cup of water.

"Here," she offered, "drink this before I make a mess of it."

I managed a few sips. She placed the cup on the floor and lay back down, carefully tucking the bottom of her clothes above the knee.

"I can't believe you ever argued with Siddhartha. How did that happen?"

"We had our disagreements, but he always had the last word. He was the most intelligent man I have ever known."

"And the others," Kisa asked, "did they ever have disputes?"

"Indeed. They've had some epic disagreements—not just little scandals that come and go, but hurtful, divisive words that almost ripped the Sangha in two. Siddhartha always said it would be nuns who would ruin the order, but it was the monks who argued and the nuns who brought peace.

"Once, when Siddhartha was staying at Kosambi, some of the brothers in Benares accused Dharmaraja of speaking ill of the Tathagata, which of course was nonsense. Dharmaraja was a devout, modest, conscientious follower of Siddhartha. All he did was question the Sangha's practice of asking villagers for food. He didn't believe it was fair to expect them to care for us." I caught my breath and continued. "I agreed with Dharmaraja, as did others. But the ones who accused him of betraying the precepts hastily decided to expel him from the order."

"That sounds absurd," Kisa exclaimed.

"That was mild compared to what happened next," I said, again stopping to catch my breath. "Dharmaraja refused to leave the order and tried to get some of the other monks to come to his aid. Before anyone knew what had happened, camps were divided between those who wanted Dharmaraja expelled and those who were on his side.

"When Siddhartha heard about the quarrel, he traveled to Benares and tried to talk some sense into the monks' skulls. By the time he arrived, both sides were accusing the other of being a disgrace to the Sangha. He listened to one group, then the other, and admonished all of them for acting like squabbling children. He thought he had succeeded in stopping their foolishness, but as soon as he was gone he heard that the factions were performing separate rituals and practices."

It sounded like Kisa had fallen asleep. "Kisa, are you awake?"

"Yes. What did he do then?"

"He didn't have a clue, so he went and spoke with Sariputta and Pajapati. Even though others saw him as the Buddha, Siddhartha often relied on his stepmother for advice and encouragement, as did I. She was present during some of my darkest days." I could almost smell Pajapati's honey-almond scent as I spoke.

"The first thing Pajapati said, after hearing about the situation, was that this kind of thing was inevitable. Then she made two suggestions, both of which Sariputta agreed with. The first was to inform the lay disciples in Benares that they should refuse to support or feed either faction until they resolved their differences. The second was that Siddhartha should speak with them all together, not separately.

"Siddhartha thought her counsel wise and asked her to instruct the lay disciples and see if that was sufficient, before speaking to both sides. It was only a matter of weeks after the lay disciples and townsfolk refused to support or honor the bhikkhus that both factions asked Siddhartha for an audience."

"He told them a story, right?" Kisa said.

"You guessed it. That man could tell a tale like no other. He could mesmerize his audience and take them where he wanted them to go." I rubbed my eyes and continued. "I don't know how he did it, but it did the trick." I yawned.

"After gathering both factions he said, 'There was a powerful king named Brahmadatta of Kasi who resided near Benares. He decided to attack the small neighboring kingdom of Kosala and make it part of his own. The king of Kosala, Dighiti, knew his small army was no match for Brahmadatta, so he took his wife and fled. They went to Benares and lived in a potter's home outside of town. They lived there a number of years, never revealing who they were to anyone outside their family. The queen gave birth to a son whom they named Dighavu.

"In fear of being discovered, King Dighiti sent his son away to be educated and skilled in all the arts. Not long after Dighavu left Benares, King Dighiti's former barber happened to see the king and reported his whereabouts to Brahmadatta. Brahmadatta, who had worried for years about King Dighiti seeking revenge, promptly had him and his wife arrested.

"While being led through the streets to their execution, King Dighiti and his wife saw their son Dighavu, who had just returned, in the crowd. Not wishing to let his son's presence be known, but wanting desperately to pass him a message, he shouted, 'My son! Do not look too far or too near. Hatred is not vanquished by hatred. Hatred is only appeased by non-hatred.'"

I yawned again.

"Please," Kisa said, "this is too tiring. Tell me the rest tomorrow."

"I'd rather finish now. I'm not sure what tomorrow will bring."

She laid her hand on my arm. She could see that the sockets around my eyes were receding.

"Siddhartha could be so dramatic," I went on. "He could shock, confuse, or enlighten you by the tone of his voice.

"After King Dighiti and his wife…," I interrupted myself. "He always said 'his wife.' Didn't she have a name? Anyway, after the couple was executed, their son Dighavu went into the forest and drank and wept for weeks on end. He remembered his father's admonition while being led to his death and vowed to come to a complete understanding of what his father had been trying to convey.

"King Brahmadatta heard that there was a son who had survived and lived in constant fear that one day he would be assassinated. He did all in his power to discover the whereabouts of King Dighiti's heir. His soldiers' searched for many years, to no avail.

"It came to pass that Dighavu heard that King Brahmadatta required some assistants for the royal elephants' stable. He applied and was granted the position, nobody knowing his true identity. He was devout, kind, responsible, and hard-working. It wasn't long before he moved into the inner circles of the palace and the confidence of the king.

"One day, while the king was hunting in the jungles, he and the king became separated from the others. After searching for their party for sometime and becoming quite tired, the king entrusted Dighavu to look after him while he slept.

"The moment Dighavu had been waiting for had finally arrived. The man who had ordered his parents death was now lying helplessly before him. He took out his sword and was about to swing when he remembered his father's last wish. Realizing this was not what his father would have wanted, he sheathed his sword and sat back down.

"The king awoke suddenly and told Dighavu that he had had a bad dream. He told him about King Dighiti, his wife, and their son, who he feared would one day seek revenge and slay him.

"Dighavu took out his sword and said, 'I am the one whom you fear. It is my father and mother that you executed.'

"King Brahmadatta pleaded for his life. Dighavu laid his sword on the ground and repeated the words of his father. 'Hatred is not vanquished by hatred. Hatred is only appeased by non-hatred.'

"The king was touched with such remorse and forgiveness that he returned the kingdom and land of King Dighiti to his son and vowed to protect and support Dighavu with his very life."

I turned onto my side and put my arm around Kisa. "After Siddhartha finished his story, Dharmaraja and those who had tried to expel him all bowed before Siddhartha, then to one another, and closed the divide they had created. That was the last major disagreement I can remember." I closed my eyes and snuggled closer to Kisa. "But I'm sure there will be more."

Kisa put her arm over my prominent ribs, as I fitfully wandered into a nomadic sleep.

Fifteen

Ambapali stopped to rest at Savatthi's Eastern Gardens. Nearing eighty, Savatthi maintained her promise to the Buddha by providing food, clothing, and medicine for every bhikkhu who came her way. She and Ambapali had been especially concerned about the bhikkhunis' lack of privacy and clothes and had conspired before Savatthi had approached the Tathagata.

They had been certain he would grant her requests, not only because of his sincere concern for all bhikkhus, but also because of his underlying belief that women were one of the greatest culprits of desire, lust, and thereby attachment, in the world. By allowing Savatthi to provide extra bathing clothes for the bhikkhunis, Siddhartha thought the monks would be less distracted and enticed. He never considered that naked men were just as tempting and distracting to his women followers.

Upon hearing of Ambapali's arrival, Savatthi rose from her afternoon nap, ordered servants to make tea and cakes, and made her way to the garden.

They placed their hands together in greeting and embraced. Savatthi exclaimed, "My old friend. What a pleasure."

"It is my joy to see you again," replied Ambapali, as she bent and rubbed her knees. "But I find no pleasure in these aching knees."

"Sit, sit," Savatthi insisted. "Stretch your legs."

Ambapali lowered herself to the blanket that was provided. Savatthi sat and began rubbing Ambapali's legs.

"You shouldn't be traveling," Savatthi said, aware of the swelling in her friend's knees, "especially this time of year. The monsoons are predicted any day now. You could get drenched or worse."

"I must," Ambapali replied.

"What is so important that you are putting your body, your divine temple, in such danger?" Savatthi demanded. "And where are your sisters? Who is assisting you?"

"Calm down," Ambapali smiled, as she touched the sleeve of her friend's sari.

"These are awful," Savatthi said loudly, referring to Ambapali's knees. Turning to a maid nearby she said, "Bring me some peppermint oil."

As the maid ran off to fetch the oil, another arrived with the tea and cakes. Savatthi stopped rubbing and gave Ambapali a cup of hot tea.

"It's Yasodhara," Ambapali said, after downing the tea in a single motion and refilling her cup. "She's dying."

"We're all dying, my friend. Look at these old bodies of clay." She waved her hand. "It's inevitable."

"Yes," Ambapali replied, "everything changes. Nothing remains. But Yasodhara, as we know her, will soon pass away. I must see her." She looked away. "There are things left unsaid."

"Isn't she living near Rajagaha?" Ambapali nodded. "That's another week's journey, at least. And that's only if you're young and strong and have healthy knees." She looked at Ambapali's legs once again.

"Blessings, my friend, but your concern is unfounded. I have traveled much farther in my days and in worse conditions."

"Yes," Savatthi replied, "ten or twenty years ago!"

The maid came back with the oil and handed the bottle to Savatthi. She poured some on her palm and began rubbing it into Ambapali's joints. After a few moments she said, "At least let me provide you with a cart and driver."

"Your kindness touches me deeply, but really, I'll be fine."

"I insist," Savatthi smiled sternly. "How could I live with myself knowing that you may be injured or sick and I could have prevented it? What would all the Buddhas say if they knew I let a living Bodhisattva walk away from my garden without proper protection and care?"

"OK, OK," Ambapali surrendered. "Your wish is my pleasure."

Savatthi finished rubbing Ambapali's aching joints and handed her some cakes.

They ate mindfully—aware of moving their hands, raising the food to their mouths, placing it between their lips, lowering their hands, tasting the sweetness on their tongues, chewing, breathing, swallowing, breathing, thinking about taking another bite, aware of each muscle strain or body ache, breathing, thoughts arising from their past, breathing, chewing, swallowing, noticing the desire to speak before words left their mouths, exhaling, seeing their mind drift before the next inhalation.

"Remember when we used to sing?" Savatthi grinned.

"It drove him crazy," Ambapali recalled. "He thought it was distracting and self-absorbent."

"I thought it was beautiful and enlightening."

"We sing sutras all the time now. At least the nuns do."

Ambapali begin to sing. Savatthi joined her.

> "Not mine and not of me,
>   The self I do not mind!
>   Thus Mara, I tell thee,
>   My path you can not find."

Their words and vibrations drifted on the breeze as they sat in the pregnant silence.

"He could be so like a man," Savatthi broke the silence, "so much order and control. He could be so compassionate and understanding, and then make a bunch of ridiculous rules and regulations."

"It wasn't easy," Ambapali replied thoughtfully. "He was butting heads with a system that's been intact for centuries. If he'd insisted on accepting us right away, with equal rights and responsibilities, he probably would have been thrown out of every town he visited. I think he did as much as he could, considering the time and place."

"Don't forget," Savatthi added, "he was raised as a man, in a man's world, with all the privileges and expectations that entails."

"You speak with great understanding," Ambapali replied, "with great compassion and wisdom."

"It is you who shows me the way," Savatthi said. "Your presence is like a cool refreshing drink." She lifted her head and sang.

> "As an act of pure devotion
> She has done a pious deed;
> She has attained salvation,
> Being free from selfish greed."

They watched their minds give birth to thoughts and feelings until Savatthi broke the silence. "They're making up stories now that he's dead."

"I know," Ambapali replied.

"Just last week I overheard some senior bhikkhus who had stopped here in the garden. They told some novices that the Buddha knew what was happening with someone who was hundreds of leagues away! And then," she almost spit, "then they said that Sariputta had walked on water, across the river south of Ribala, to hear the Blessed One's words."

"What?"

"This so-called 'brother' says to the novice, 'It is well known that Our Lord, the Tathagata, could ascertain someone's heart even when they were not physically present.' When I heard that I knew I was in for a good one and stayed hidden in the shadows. He said, 'The Lord Buddha was at Jetavana, in the city of Sravasti, delivering the Dharma to twelve hundred bhikkhus and lay disciples. Among the crowd were the great Sariputra, Maudgalyayana, Kaustila, Purna Metaluniputra, Subhut, and Umpanishada.'

"I knew right away he was full of it. The only time all of them were together was at the Buddha's bedside before his death," Savatthi said. "You were there." Ambapali nodded.

"He said, 'The Lord Buddha and all those in attendance were invited to join a special feast by Prasenajit, the King of Sravasti, who was celebrating the anniversary of his father's death. Our Lord accepted the king's invitation and he and all those present at Jetavana followed him to King Prasenajit's royal grounds.

"'Ananda, who had been in another province on matters of the Sangha, returned to Jetavana to find an empty encampment. Not knowing where everyone had gone, he decided to take his bowl and ask for alms.

"'While going door to door he came upon the house of Maudenka, a prostitute, who had a beautiful daughter name Pchiti. Upon seeing the handsome face of Ananda, Pchiti fell in love and asked her mother to cast a spell over his person to make him her own.'

"You should have seen the faces on these young men," Savatthi grinned, "they were enraptured.

"He continued, 'The charm worked immediately and Ananda found himself inside their home entering Pchiti's bedroom.'

"Now, listen to this," Savatthi exclaimed. "He says, 'The Tathagata, who had returned to the Jeta Grove after King Prasenajit's feast, went into samadhi and saw Ananda's temptation. He called for Majusri and told him of Ananda's whereabouts. He asked Majusri to go and rescue Ananda from the woman's spell.

"'Upon arriving at the home of Maudenka, Majusri entered, cast off the charm, and brought Ananda back to his senses and the Dharma.'

"Ha!" Savatthi blurted. "See what I mean?"

"The Tathagata always discounted such nonsense," Ambapali replied.

"I know," Savatthi stammered. "I couldn't believe it. I almost got up and punched the idiot right then and there, but couldn't. I wanted to hear what he would come up with next."

"You know," Ambapali smiled, "sometimes Siddhartha, excuse me, the Tathagata, didn't know what we were saying or thinking even when we were right in front of his face, let alone somewhere else."

"I know!" Savatthi said. "But that's not all. Wait until you hear this.

"After the adoration for his previous tale died down he starts again. 'The world-honored Buddha...'

"World-honored?" Savatthi interrupted herself. "He got around, but I doubt he's known around the world! Anyway, he said, 'The world-honored one sat by a river and preached to the villagers of a hamlet south of Bodhi Gaya, but they were not easily convinced. Sariputta, having heard that the Lord Buddha was in the vicinity, wanted to meet this glorious teacher and hear the Truth for himself. He set out to join them but found that he was on the opposite side of the river. Not knowing how to swim and seeing that the water was swift and wide, he could not fathom how he would reach the other shore.

"'Finally, being overcome by his devotion to hear the Blessed One, he told himself that somehow he would get there if he believed hard enough and had faith. Without thinking, he stepped forward. He walked across the surface of the river and approached the villagers and Lord Buddha.

"'When the crowd saw Sariputta step ashore, his clothes dry as a bone, they asked how he was able to cross without a boat. He said it was because of his faith in the Tathagata that he had arrived without drowning or getting wet.

"'The Tathagata said Saripuuta had spoken the truth. 'Faith can save the world from constant migration and deliver us from death.'"

"Wow!" Ambapali exclaimed. "I could use something like that now to get to Rajagaha."

"It's not funny," Savatthi cautioned. "This is how rumors become legends."

"I know," Ambapali said seriously. "What did you do?"

"Not wanting to shame him in front of the others," she explained, "I took the elder aside the next morning before he departed and told him a thing or two...or three or four. I told him his stories were rubbish and did nothing but hurt the Sangha and the Dharma. I told him that the Tathagata had always disapproved of magic and superstition and said if I ever heard him propagating such lies again I would personally strip off his robe, throw him in the river, and tell him to walk to the other side!"

"I will stop upon my return," Ambapali said, as she prepared to leave. "You bring me such joy."

"The pleasure has been mine," Savatthi replied.

"Because of your kindness and generosity, my chances of seeing Yasodhara before she passes has increased ten-fold."

"It should only take two to three days with the cart and driver," Savatthi replied. "If that is not soon enough, then it was not meant to be."

"Namasté."

"Namasté," Savatthi replied. "May all the Bodhisattvas and sentient beings hold you in the palm of their hands."

"And you."

Ambapali waved, leaning back on the soft pillows
Savatthi had provided in the wagon. She smiled broadly,
placed her hands together, and bowed. From a distance she
saw Savatthi do the same.

Sixteen

Ananda made his way through the center of town to the grounds of Devadatta's luxurious home. Devadatta, like other provisional officials and descendants of royal Brahmins, held court under a large white tent in his garden. Incense burned in front of the Vedic gods sitting sternly at the entrance, reminding those with frivolous matters to keep away.

Scurrying clerks and servants served tea and sweets to visitors and escorted townspeople with grievances, requests, or petitions into and out of the tent. Devadatta and his fellow officials sat and listened to the stream of humanity in the early morning and evening, before and after the withering heat of the day. Long lines gathered at dawn, people waiting three to four hours for their turn, if they got an audience at all. If not, they had to return the next day.

When Ananda arrived, the sun was just beginning to laugh at the night and take away its cloak of darkness. There were already dozens before him.

As he stood waiting he tried to meditate, but seeing him robed as a monk, people kept approaching and asking for his blessings. He did not refuse. As the line behind him grew and the morning sun rose in the sky, he feared he may have to return in the evening.

He began questioning his decision and contemplated how he would present his request to Devadatta without

sounding desperate or demanding. As he wiped beads of
sweat from his brow, he thought of Savatthi and her skill at
presenting her request to care for the Sangha to the Buddha.
She had made it sound as if she was doing it all for others,
without any thought of personal gain, until Gotama had
asked her what her true motivations were. When she said it
would also bring her good karma and happiness he had
granted her request.

Perhaps he should do the same. He was doing this as
much for Devadatta as he was for himself. Most importantly,
he was waiting in line for the sake of Yasodhara and her son.
Thinking of Yasodhara reminded him of his audience with
Gotama after he had been discovered by Majusri at the home
of Maudenka, the prostitute.

He was having tea with Maudenka and her
daughter Pchiti. Being most gracious, they had invited
him inside, out of the afternoon heat.

Majusri knocked and ask Maudenka if they had
seen him, as it was reported he had passed that way
earlier in the day. Ananda heard his name and went
to the door. Majusri, upon seeing Ananda in the
presence of Maudenka, suppressed his shock and
informed Ananda that he had been summoned by
the Tathagata. Majusri didn't know that Maudenka
and Pchiti had been discussing the possibility of
joining the Sangha. All he knew was that Ananda,
one of the most trusted devotees of the Lord Buddha,
had compromised himself by entering a home of
desire.

Majusri didn't speak to Ananda on their way back
to the Jeta Grove, but when they arrived he went
straight to Gotama and told him where he had found
Ananda.

Gotama asked Ananda if it was true that he was being entertained at the home of Maudenka.

"Yes, Lord," he had replied, "although I wouldn't say 'entertained.' I was instructing Maudenka and her daughter Pchiti in the Dharma."

Everyone in the grove was listening, waiting for an explanation from this most virtuous of bhikkhus.

"They wish to become arahats and follow the Eightfold Path," he explained. "They invited me in, out of the sun, to question our religious life and practices. If I have offended the Tathagata or the Sangha, I apologize and humbly ask for forgiveness." He then proceeded to kneel and touch his head to the floor.

"Thou has offended no one, my dear Ananda," the Buddha replied. "Sharing the Dharma with those caught in illusion is one of the noblest acts a bhikkhu can perform."

Upon hearing the Tathagata's words, Majusri bowed before Ananda and said, "Forgive me, brother. I am the one who was captured by Mara, caught in my own judgments and illusions."

"There is nothing to forgive," Ananda responded with a smile. "You devoutly reported what you had witnessed, wishing only to help me on my path, to keep me from falling into worldliness and temptation."

Ananda and Majusri turned and faced the Buddha. "Although I must admit," Ananda grinned sheepishly, "Maudenka's daughter is quite beautiful. Lustful thoughts did cross my mind. To say otherwise would be a lie."

"Thoughts and feelings come and go," Gotama said. "It is our intentions that create heaven or hell, our actions that continue the cycle of cause and effect."

"Hey!" Ananda heard someone yelling. "Are you deaf?"

An administrative assistant was standing before him. He was at the front of the line. He looked back and realized that he was the last person being allowed in that morning.

"I said, what's your name?"

"Forgive me," he stuttered. "I am known as Ananda, a follower of the Buddha from Gotama."

"Wait here," the man said, hurrying into the tent and returning quickly. "Follow me."

"Here is Ananda," the man proclaimed, standing to the side, as Ananda came front and center before Devadatta and the other administrators.

"Ananda?" Devadatta bellowed. "What are you doing here?" He started to rise with alarm. "Is it Yasodhara?"

"Yes. No!" Ananda said quickly. "She's OK, at the moment."

Devadatta sat back down and grunted with annoyance. He didn't like to have his apprehension and concern so visibly seen in front of others. "Well," he said, "what do you want?"

"It is most urgent," Ananda explained. "May I speak to you in private?"

Devadatta looked left and right. Without a word, his colleagues began leaving, taking the opportunity to go home early and rest or have a drink before returning for the evenings session.

After everyone was gone, Ananda stepped onto the raised platform and sat on a pillow. With a practiced and adamant tone he said, "Your sister is dying."

"I know that!" Devadatta said impatiently. "You interrupted me for that?"

"No," Ananda continued. "It will be soon. It could be any day."

Devadatta sat back limply on his pillows. Sadness invaded his eyes.

"How do you know?" he asked, challenging Ananda's prediction.

"I have seen hundreds of monks and nuns pass away from similar ailments. She is losing strength and has lost her appetite. It won't be long until she can not get out of bed."

Devadatta looked gravely into the distance.

"I'm afraid," Ananda said quietly, "that Rahula will not arrive in time."

"Yes," Devadatta replied faintly. "I heard that you summoned him."

"That was over two months ago," Ananda said.

"What do you expect me to do?"

"Find him."

"What? He could be anywhere!"

"No, not anywhere," Ananda replied. "He's traveling from Sri Lanka. Surely he is coming up the valley through the pass, traveling with his wife and son. His son is about nine or eleven by now."

"There are thousands of travelers between here and there. You ask me to do the impossible."

Ananda heard the conviction in Devadatta's voice wavering and saw the wheels turning in his knitted brow.

"He must be getting close and you are the only one who will recognize him. You are the only one I can trust. I must stay here and care for Yasodhara and guide the Sangha," Ananda explained. "You must leave now...today!"

Devadatta stood proudly and proclaimed, "Yes. You were right to come. I will get horses, men, and provisions and leave before night falls." It felt good to be "doing something" he thought, instead of hovering around like a jackal waiting for his sister to die. "I must speak with Chitra."

Ananda followed Devadatta towards the exit. Devadatta stopped abruptly, turned, and bowed. "Thank you," he said softly. "Thank you for being my sister's friend."

"It is I who am blessed with good fortune by her presence," Ananda replied, "and yours."

"It's so ironic," thought Ananda, as he left Devadatta and made his way to my hut. "After all these years, with her body decaying before me I still find she attracts me like no other." He grinned. "If Majusri and Gotama saw my thoughts now they would realize that any desire I had for Maudenka and her daughter Pchiti were like mud puddles compared to the rivers of passion that Yasodhara awakens in my heart."

Seventeen

"Catch me if you can!" Bodhi yelled, his newfound friend Jitaka close behind, straining to grab him as they ran up the trail. Light traces of snow could be seen on the approaching mountaintops.

"Stay to the side!" Rahula cautioned, "away from the edge!" The boys were oblivious, like two sure-footed deer prancing haphazardly up and down the steep slopes.

"Jitaka!" his mother screamed. "Get back here!" His mother's command stopped Jitaka in his tracks, but Bodhi kept running. Savarna walked alongside Jitaka's mother Mirabi and laughed. How many times had she yelled at Bodhi to stop, slow down, come back, or stay put? She'd lost track.

They were two days into the mountains, traveling with a family they'd met in the foothills. Mirabi's father, Ramu, was walking with Rahula, slightly ahead of the women. Ramu, whose people were from Videha, spoke with Rahula, who was always looking ahead, keeping an eye on his son.

"Yes, yes," Ramu insisted, "you must know the forest like your wife, every clearing and pathway." Ramu had been hunting since he was a boy. When Rahula eventually confessed that he, too, had been a hunter, Ramu recited a litany of close encounters, thrills, and successes. "If you don't," Ramu continued, "it can be your death. Just like marriage," he chuckled. Rahula forced a grin and nodded.

"For example," Ramu testified, as they walked up a ridge that leveled off on a plateau, "surely you've noticed my limp?" Rahula nodded. It was impossible to miss the short stiff steps Ramu took with his right leg.

"It was a tiger—a Bengali tiger the size of an elephant." Rahula had grown accustomed to Ramu's "slight" exaggerations.

"We were in the forests northeast of Gotama—five of us, with one elephant, a horse, bows, and spears. We'd been following the devil for four days. It had already killed two of the children in our village. One little girl got dragged away from the well. The other poor child had been separated from his family on their way home from a funeral, of all things." Rahula looked ahead, making sure Bodhi was in sight.

"I'd never seen such tracks. You could fit two men's feet inside one print. We knew this was no ordinary cat and, I've got to admit, I was scared."

Rahula realized he couldn't see Bodhi and walked faster. The old man picked up his step. Savarna, Mirabi, and Jitaka followed.

"What's the rush?" Mirabi called.

"Bodhi?!" Rahula screamed. "Bodhi?!" There was no answer. He started running, leaving Ramu behind. He ran through a small grove of trees and looked down the path. "Bodhi?!" he yelled. "This isn't funny. Where are you?"

"He's right here," a voice snarled.

Some men stepped clear of the trees. One of them was holding Bodhi with an arm around his waist and a hand covering his mouth. Bodhi struggled like a fish out of water, but the man had a tight grip.

"Let him go!" Rahula said, approaching Bodhi's capturers. "I said, let him go!" He moved closer but two of the men, wearing coats of fur, picked him up and threw him to the ground.

Ramu, Mirabi, Jitaka, and Savarna rounded the corner just as Rahula, who had crawled towards Bodhi, was kicked in the side and fell on his back, the wind knocked out of his lungs. Savarna couldn't speak.

"Oh, how fortunate," the man holding Bodhi exclaimed. "More people means more money."

Ramu half-ran half-limped towards the man holding Bodhi. As he approached, one of the other men drew a long knife and Ramu froze. Mirabi and Jitaka stayed put as Savarna helped Rahula off the ground. They could see that Bodhi had stopped struggling and wasn't harmed.

"What do you want?" Savarna said, as Rahula's breath returned.

"You don't look bad," the man holding Bodhi grinned. "But not to worry, we'll leave enough for your little brother and grandpa to clean up." He nodded towards Rahula and Ramu.

"Let him go and we'll give you whatever you want," Savarna said coldly.

"Anything we want...now let me think." He looked at Mirabi, Ramu, Rahula, and Savarna. "From the looks of you I doubt you have much money, but I've been wrong before."

Mirabi reached inside her sari and took out her money belt. "Here!" she said, throwing it at the bandits' feet. "Take it. It's all we have."

"Don't mind if I do," said the ringleader. He passed Bodhi to the man standing nearby, picked up the money belt, and counted the contents. "Not bad. Not bad at all," he said, "but not good enough."

"Let the boy go," Ramu insisted.

"I believe there's more here than meets the eye, old man," the bandit winked. "Do we have to strip you all to find what's left?"

Savarna handed over her bracelets, Rahula gave them his ring, and Ramu bent down and placed a bag of rupees at their feet.

"We have nothing left," Rahula insisted.

"You have something much more valuable than money, my friend," the bandit said, shaking the valuables in his hand and staring at Savarna and Mirabi.

"If you hurt my boy or touch them, one of you will die before I do," Rahula promised, blood rushing to his face as his knees shook.

The leader smiled. "I wouldn't make threats if I were you; you might have to back them up."

The men who had thrown Rahula to the ground grabbed Savarna and dragged her towards the trees. She screamed, hit them in the face, kicked at their feet, and bit their hands. Bodhi and Mirabi cried out. Rahula and Ramu ran towards the men dragging Savarna but were knocked down by the other bandits. As they picked themselves off the ground, the thieves shook their heads and pulled out their knives.

"I warned you," the ringleader said.

Ramu advanced undeterred but was swiftly stabbed in the shoulder and fell. Rahula deflected the leader's slash at his throat and pounded him in the jaw. When he hit the ground, Rahula kicked the knife away but was grabbed by the leg and pulled down.

The men dragging Savarna towards the trees saw their headman on the ground and ran to help. The man holding Bodhi released his grip and joined the fray.

As Ramu lay moaning and the bandits went to back up their fallen leader, Mirabi took Jitaka into the forest to hide. Savarna grabbed a rock and ran to help Rahula.

As the bandits closed in for the kill, men on horseback galloped across the plateau. The horses were heard before being seen. The bandits paused, but Savarna didn't. She hit the man closest to her with the rock. He fell limply, blood oozing from his temple. She turned and saw riders with raised spears and bows bearing down upon them. Savarna crouched next to Rahula and covered their heads, not knowing if they were going to be killed by the bandits or the horsemen.

The bandits scattered, leaving everything they'd stolen and the unconscious thief.

Arrows flew overhead, just missing their mark, as the thieves fled into the woods. One of the men was struck in the leg. He screamed, reaching for his thigh, but kept running until he was out of sight.

Savarna helped Rahula stand. He clasped his side. Some ribs were broken. Bodhi, after being released, ran to help his parents, grabbed their waists, and wouldn't let go.

Ramu moaned. Savarna and Rahula made their way to where he lay as Mirabi and Jitaka emerged from hiding and ran to her father's side.

The riders stopped chasing the bandits, trotted back, and looked upon the surviving and wounded travelers with curiosity and concern.

"Ahhhhh," Ramu yelled. "Leave me alone! I'll be fine." Mirabi was helping him up. He swaying slightly and held his shoulder; his jacket was soaked in blood.

"Put a bandage on that," one of the horsemen instructed another, pointing at Ramu's shoulder. The man leapt off of his horse, pulled out a pack, and took out some cloth. He pushed back Ramu's shirt and applied the bandage. Ramu grimaced, but made no sound.

The travelers bowed, shielded their eyes from the glaring sun, and looked up at the rider's faces.

"How can we ever repay you?" Rahula said, speaking for all.

"By coming with me to see your mother," a vaguely familiar voice bellowed.

Eighteen

The riders dismounted. Rahula strained to see the man who had spoken, wondering how he knew his mother.

"Rahula," Devadatta exclaimed, "you don't recognize me?" He pulled the hair on his face. "Perhaps you don't remember me with so much gray?"

Rahula looked closely at the eyes smiling upon him like a shining star.

"Uncle!" They embraced, oblivious to those around them, tears falling freely.

"I can't believe it," Devadatta said, admiring his nephew. "You've grown into such a fine young man." He turned towards Savarna and Bodhi. "And this must be your wife and son?"

"Savarna and Bodhi," he said, then turned around, "and these are our friends Ramu, his daughter Mirabi, and her son Jitaka."

Devadatta nodded, then referred proudly back to his nephew. "I've known him since he was just a sprout."

"You arrived at an opportune time uncle. A few more minutes and you would have found a dead nephew."

"We saw you from the ridge," Devadatta explained. "We weren't sure what was going on, but as we got closer we got a good idea."

"What brings you this way and what did you say about his mother?" Ramu nodded at Rahula.

"His mother is ill," Devadatta said. "Very ill." He looked at Rahula, hoping he understood. Rahula stared back blankly, then realized the implication. "We have extra horses and a cart. I insist that you join us," Devadatta commanded Ramu and his family, who bowed with gratitude.

"Ananda says it's getting close," Devadatta whispered to Rahula, as he helped his nephew onto the mares back.

"How would he know?" Rahula asked.

"He's been caring for her, along with her cousin Kisa. Chitra and I have done what we can."

"What's your mother-in-law like?" Mirabi asked Savarna as Devadatta's men brought the cart down from the ridge, gathered their belongings, and helped them settle in.

"I don't know; we've never met."

"Never?"

"Never."

"Where's she from?" Mirabi inquired. "Who is her family?"

"She's from the same area as your father—Gotama. Her father's name is Suprabuddha."

Ramu, who was groggy with pain, suddenly interrupted. "Suprabuddha from Kali?"

"I believe so, yes."

"Well, well," Ramu grinned, shaking his head.

"What is it, Father?" Mirabi asked. "Who is Suprabuddha?"

Savarna looked at Rahula and Devadatta, then told herself, "What if they know? It's nothing to be ashamed of."

"Suprabuddha's daughter is Yasodhara," Ramu explained.

"Yasodhara?" Mirabi puzzled. "Sounds familiar."

"The wife of the Buddha," he said. "Gotama."

Mirabi looked at Savarna, then stared at Rahula, who was perched behind his uncle. "He's the son of the Buddha?" she exclaimed.

Savarna nodded.

"Didn't he die a long time ago?" .

"Not that long ago," Ramu corrected. "As I recall, his wife, your mother-in-law," he addressed Savarna, "was also a nun, right?"

"Yes," Savarna replied, just as Devadatta and Rahula came alongside. "Please don't say anything. He doesn't like people to know." Ramu and Mirabi nodded their consent.

"You'll have quite a story to tell your grandchildren and the scar to prove it," Rahula shouted to Ramu, referring to the bandits.

"I will indeed," Ramu grinned. "I'll have the story of a lifetime."

Nineteen

"Grandfather," Jitaka asked, "who is this Buddha man?" He and Bodhi had been listening to the conversation in the back of the cart and had waited until Rahula and Devadatta rode ahead.

"The Buddha of Gotama is one of the greatest men I have ever had the pleasure to meet. Your grandfather," Ramu addressed Bodhi, "was a wise and compassionate man. I also remember his father; your great-grandfather, King Suddhodana."

"My great-grandfather was a king?" Bodhi asked.

"He was indeed," Ramu replied, "but when your grandfather left home he changed. He became bitter and melancholy. Ouch!" Ramu winced, grabbing his shoulder as the cart bumped violently over a deep rut.

"Father!" Mirabi stood, almost losing her balance. "Are you all right?" She laid her hand gently near his wound.

"I'm fine," he replied. "Leave me alone."

She sat back down after assuring herself that he was OK.

"About six or seven years after he'd left home," Ramu continued, pushing aside his pain, "the Buddha returned to Kapilavatthu and went to see his father. At first the old man refused to see him, but his wife Pajapati, your great-grandmother," he once again addressed Bodhi, "talked him into having an audience with his son." Ramu rubbed his shoulder. "After hearing his son's reasons for leaving and the wisdom he had gained, the king's heart softened. He allowed the Buddha, his son, who had been known as Prince Siddhartha, to teach in the village the very next day."

"My grand-father was a prince?" Bodhi exclaimed.

"I was privileged to hear him speak in the village on that very day." Ramu bent his head in reflection, then continued. "Your mother, bless her," he said to Mirabi, "she's the one who convinced me to go." Mirabi shared the grief in her father's eyes when he mentioned her mother. "I wasn't going to listen to some spiritual mumbo jumbo from a young tyke I'd known since he was a baby," he grinned, "but your mother said she had heard great things about Siddhartha and that he was a changed man. I tried to get out of it," he laughed. "I had a plan to get up early and go work in the fields, but she got up before me and stood at the door with a pack and some water, ready to go." He could almost see his wife's stubborn expression.

Bodhi turned to Savarna. "Grandfather was a prince!"

Savarna nodded and turned back to Ramu. "What happened at the gathering?"

"It was a good thing I'd gotten up early. When we arrived it was packed. I have never seen so many people at once, except for the religious festival that's held once every seven years."

He shifted his feet and braced himself as the cart swayed side to side or bounced up into the air. "Your grandfather had grown in body and stature. He was one of the best looking men I'd ever seen, though I'm not a great judge of handsome," he chuckled. "But there was far more to him than his looks. There was something about his presence. We were a stone's throw from where he sat, yet it felt like he was right next to us. He was peaceful, tranquil, undisturbed by people, places, and things."

"What do you mean?" Savarna asked.

"It was as if nothing in the world existed except that moment. I had no desire to do anything other than sit in his presence. And when he spoke...his words melted your heart like soft cream."

The driver of the cart shouted, not able to hear their conversation. "It's getting late. We'll be stopping to set up camp soon." They looked at the horizon and realized the truth of his words.

"Please," Savarna said, impervious to the approaching darkness, "what did he say?"

"He told a story; a story about karma and evil." The boys edged closer, eager to forget their earlier misadventure.

Ramu leaned forward. "He said that misery arises from vain, pride-filled people committing evil acts towards others. He had witnessed the ignorance and harsh words of such people and felt nothing but compassion for their foolishness. He said that if someone harmed him, he would respond with 'ungrudging love.' He said that the more evil directed at him, the greater amount of goodness he would show in return.

"As if on cue, a man from a distant province began shouting abuse and hurtling insults at the Buddha. He thought he was a big phony and told him so. Others in the crowd tried to silence the man, but the Buddha insisted he be allowed to continue. When the gentleman paused to catch his breath, the Buddha calmly asked, 'If a man declined to accept a present given to him, to whom would it belong?'

"The man replied, 'It would belong to the man who offered it, you idiot. What do you think?'

"The Buddha then said, 'You have spewed your venom at me, but I decline to accept it and request that you keep it for yourself. Will it not be a source of misery to thee? Just like the echo belongs to the sound and the shadow to the substance, so misery will overtake the evildoer without fail.' Then he said, 'A wicked man who reproaches a man who is fully awake and compassionate is like one who looks up and spits at heaven; the spittle soils not the heaven, but comes back and defiles his own person. It is like one who flings dust at another when the wind is contrary; the dust does but return on him who threw it. The awakened man cannot be hurt and the misery that the other would inflict comes back on himself.'"

"What happened?" Jitaka asked. "Did the man attack the Buddha?"

"No," Ramu laughed. "The man didn't know what to stay and went away in a rage. I heard that he returned the following day and joined the Buddha and his followers."

Savarna was touched by the words her father-in-law had spoken.

"Did you talk to him?" Bodhi asked.

"No," Ramu grinned. "There were thousands of people. I was too far away." He shook his head. "I don't know what I would have said. That man was as sharp as a knife."

"Did you become a decipole?" Bodhi asked.

"A disciple," Savarna corrected.

"No, no," Ramu professed. "I'm not one to get involved in groups, especially religious stuff like that. It was beyond me." He paused. "But I'll tell you this," his eyes rested on Bodhi, "your grandfather will be known throughout the coming ages."

The cart stopped. They looked forward and saw Rahula and Devadatta approaching.

"Looks like this is where we'll be setting up camp," said the driver.

As they pulled on their shawls and blankets against the chilled air and got out of the cart to gather their things, Savarna whispered to Ramu, "What about Yasodhara?"

"What about her?" Ramu replied, as his daughter helped him to the ground.

"Where was she?" Savarna wondered. "When you went and listened to the Buddha, wasn't she there?"

"I don't know," Ramu said, wincing from the pain in his shoulder. "Does it matter?"

"No, I guess not," Savarna replied, realizing he'd probably never given the Buddha's wife much thought. She took Bodhi's hand and prayed for the chance to meet Yasodhara face-to-face.

Twenty

Ananda arrived early the next morning following his usual routines. I went in and out of consciousness, seeing dim shapes and bright lights. We were aware of one another's silence and respected the need and habit to not speak.

I heard myself rambling. Ananda didn't interrupt or try to understand. He knew I was working through inner states, preparing to leave the body that had served me for so many years. I could feel life squeezing from my pores, as if there wasn't room for both of us.

"No, no!" I yelled. "Turn back. It's not safe! Look behind the trees! Go back!" My breath quickened.

After my excitement slowed down, my breath took on its previous rhythm of long exhalations mixed with spans of no breath before I inhaled again. Without warning, tears rolled down my cheeks.

My mind was playing tricks. I awoke from a nightmare in which my son and his family were attacked by demons on the top of a mountain. I screamed, but they couldn't hear. I was grateful for moments of wakefulness. Simply looking at the roof over my bed could send me spinning.

I am back with Siddhartha, feeling his restlessness and unease about my pregnancy. He's pacing the floor like a caged lion, waiting to break free. He lies beside me reassuringly, soothing my fear. My cheeks are wet with tears as his disappearance rips me apart. "What did I do?" I question. "Was it the way I looked; something I did; something I said?" I am attacked with incriminating voices and self-inflicted wounds of doubt.

Suddenly, Siddhartha disappears and the face of our newborn son awaits my attention. His presence and needs pull me out of despair. I see him growing, running, and falling on his behind; disbelief and wonder wash his face as he tries to navigate walking. Now, a young man, feeling his power, walking with confidence, causing me to look up at his newfound height.

Before long my saving grace leaves the land of his birth to find his own path, his own meaning. He finds me with the bhikkhus and tells me of his decision.

I try to persuade him. I plead, beg, make a spectacle of myself in front of the other nuns. I know his leaving has something to do with his father. He snarls "liar" and "hypocrite" during his explanation, but won't tell me what he is talking about. I can see the back of his head as he leaves, his dark hair and broad shoulders just like his fathers.

Then, I remembered. He's coming home! My sorrow turned to joy.

A pain stabbed at my heart. I rolled sideways and curled into a ball. Ananda's hand was on my back. I drifted again…

I can feel the cold, the rain, the mud, and the dirt. It's oozing through my toes, seeping into my bones. I'm shivering, wandering the countryside in nothing but a flimsy thin robe. People are offering me food and shelter, but I refuse and keep walking. I can see a light ahead, a golden light of warmth. As I get closer, it moves farther away. "Wait! Please!"

My robe is caught on a branch. I stumble and fall in the mud. I can't breathe or move. Then I'm being lifted into the air, hands under my arms, guiding me towards the light, whispering voices saying I'll get there soon enough; there is no need to hurry or fear. The hands let go. I fall back into my body, stuck in the mud, trying to rise up out of the ooze to catch my breath.

Ambapali's angelic face appears. "Here," she gives me her hand. "Let me help."

"But I'm supposed to hate you," I say.

"I know," she replies, "but I know you don't."

"No, I don't. Where are you taking me?" I wonder.

"I don't know?" Ambapali answers. "I'm not there yet."

"You're not?"

She walks ahead, slowly rising and melting into the sky.

A clanging in my ears makes me whirl around in time to jump out of the way of a large ox. I can feel its hot breath. The bell around its neck has saved me.

My eyes opened. I saw the roof and felt blood rushing through my veins. Ananda was deep in meditation. I remembered where I was. The line was so thin; it could break at any moment. Reality was as elusive as trying to hold water. My boundaries were disintegrating.

Hundreds of eyes stare, waiting for me to speak. They're boring holes into my body and hooks into my mind, trying to find answers. They want me to absolve them, make them whole. I have nothing to say, nothing to give, no way to transmit my understanding. It isn't something I can talk about or write on a scroll. They don't believe me. They say I am a teacher, an Arahat, a soul who has been awakened, but I can only see my reflection in others. It is beyond my grasp. I have become too distanced to see the Buddha in myself.

"Let me up!" I scream. "Let me up or I'll tell Mom."

"No. you won't," says Devadatta, tickling me under the arms until I think I'll wet myself.

I'm laughing so hard I'm about to cry. Out of desperation I grab some dirt and fling it in his face. He yells and falls to the ground. I jump up and run to his side. "I'm sorry. I didn't mean to hurt you."

He acts like he's in desperate misery, then suddenly takes his hands from his eyes, gives me a devilish grin, and starts tickling me again.

I laughed so hard the bed started to shake. I awoke to see Ananda had fallen asleep. My old friend looked very tired. My eyes closed.

"You'll never be free of me," Siddhartha says.

"Why would I want to?" I say calmly.

"Because you deserve it."

"I deserved you," I say. "You didn't have to leave to find yourself."

"I know that now," he says, without moving his mouth.

"I wish you would have known then what you know now," I sigh. "It would have saved us all a great deal of sorrow."

"Can you ever forgive me?"

"Siddhartha, my love," I hold his hand, "it was our karma. If you think my desire for you is keeping me bound, you are mistaken."

"They say you've kept our love burning like a fire. I don't want that fire to extinguish your chances for liberation."

"You are deluded, my dear," I kiss his cheek. "Yes, I carry you in my heart, along with thousands of others. In fact, it's getting so crowded in here my heart is about to burst."

He laughs, kisses me on the lips, and vanishes.

My arm ached. It had fallen asleep under my side. I stretched it out and felt the tingling. I bent my wrist and straightened my fingers. I observed the veins under my skin as they turned into rivers. I plunged in and swam to another world.

My mother visited often those days. She was known as Queen Trinkata.

"There you are," she says, her silver bracelets and pendants dangling from her arms and neck. "I've been looking for you."

"I've been right here," I reply, reaching out.

She kisses me right between the eyes. A wave of sunshine splashes over me.

"I love you, Mom."

"I know, dear. And we always will," she says, drifting away.

"Where are you going?"

Her lips don't move but I hear her say, "I'll see you later."

"Mom!"

When I called out, Ananda was startled awake. He looked around, wondering who spoke, then realized I was seeing and hearing people he could not see. He knew the only difference between us then was our perceptions of reality.

He saw me reach towards the ceiling with a smile on my face and tears in my eyes. He tried to connect with my vision, but couldn't. All he could see was me lying in bed calling for my mother and talking to invisible beings.

Twenty-One

When Lasha arrived in Rajagaha she went directly, without any pretense of shopping, to her daughter's home. Davidia was at his shop. She found Kisa lying in bed sobbing, just like she'd done as a little girl when something bad happened or she hadn't gotten her way.

She entered quietly and sat on the bed.

"Mother!" Kisa exclaimed. "Thank God you're here." She put her arms around her mother and drenched her sari in tears. "I can't do this."

"Do what dear?"

"Yasodhara," she sobbed. "She's dying."

Lasha looked away as she held Kisa. "But darling, it happens to us all."

"I can't live without her. There's nobody like her, nobody."

"That is true," her mother replied, "There is nobody like her."

"I can't watch it happen," Kisa said, sitting up and drying her tears with the sleeve of her wrinkled top. "I won't do it. Ananda's there during the day. She'll be fine."

"Who cares for her at night?"

"Well… " Kisa stammered, "I do."

"Is there nobody else? What about her brother and sister?"

"She wants me. She's afraid they'll take her to their house and tell her what to do."

"Will they?" Kisa didn't answer.

"Would they do that?" her mother asked again.

"They might," Kisa finally replied. "Her brother's pretty stubborn."

"Then it's up to us," Lasha said matter-of-factly.

"Us?"

"Yes, us," her mother replied. She stood and headed towards the door.

"Where are you going?"

"To see Yasodhara. Are you coming or not?"

Wordlessly they packed a basket of supplies. Kisa watched her mother affectionately. She knew if word got back to her father that her mom visited her and Yasodhara, he might lose his head and do something stupid.

Lasha insisted that her driver, Sirimor, take them to Yasodhara's. Sirimor thought about reminding her of King Bishanara's admonition to never visit Kisa, let alone anyone else, but saw her fierce resolve and helped them onto the cart.

As they rode across town Kisa told her mother about the preceding days, the possibility of Rahula's return, and Devadatta's journey to find his nephew. She told her about Ananda's devotion and his long-concealed desire to marry, which Yasodhara had confided to her the day following their walk to the garden.

"Is it safe, a man with such passions, to care for her?" Lasha asked with alarm.

"Mother," Kisa smiled, "you are so traditional."

"Traditional?" Her mother feigned injury.

"Society is changing. You have to change with the times."

"Who's with you now?" her mother replied. "Who is sitting here in broad daylight with the likes of you, openly disobeying her husband?"

She squeezed her mother's hand.

"I just don't want Yasodhara's reputation compromised," Lasha explained.

"He took care of the Buddha. Don't you think he can set aside his needs and desires at a time like this?" Her mother nodded. "Yasodhara has never cared about her reputation. And..." she sniffed, "she's so far gone now it doesn't matter anyway."

They arrived in the late afternoon as the sun was finding its way towards the western horizon. Ananda was asleep but quickly arose when he heard them enter.

"Kisa," he whispered, as Yasodhara laughed and reached skyward. "What a pleasure." He bowed. Kisa bowed back.

"This is my mother," Kisa said.

Her mother bowed to Ananda, who returned the greeting.

"I've heard that you have been taking excellent care of our mutual friend," Lasha said. "Thank you for your kindness and devotion."

"There is no place I would rather be."

"How has she been?" Kisa asked, as they all stepped outside.

Ananda noticed the adorned cart, horses, and driver, then replied, "She's traveling."

"Traveling?" Lasha said confused. "What do you mean?"

"She's going places inside, places where we can't follow."

"Does that mean she's..." Kisa hesitated, "she's about to..."

"She's much closer. It could be any day."

"Let's see if she needs anything," Lasha said, turning towards the door. Then she stopped and faced Ananda. "Kisa was right." He looked puzzled. "You are a good and honorable man."

"Thank you," Ananda replied. "I'll see you both in the morning." He turned, bowed to the driver, and walked quickly out of sight to hide his tears.

When they entered I was hanging over the side of the bed. Lasha and Kisa ran to my side and lifted my arm and leg, placing them gently back in bed under the covers. In doing so, Lasha felt the bottom blanket.

"She's wet," she whispered. "Get a dry blanket from the basket."

Kisa returned with the blanket. They carefully turned and lifted my weakening body until the wet linen had been replaced.

"Get some water and a towel," Lasha instructed her daughter.

Kisa followed her mother's instruction, knowing what to do already but needing her mother's assurance that she could handle the emotional burden.

My eyes opened. "Kisa, what are you doing way up there?" I asked.

She looked confused and turned to her mother, who said, "We just arrived. Ananda has been here all day."

"Ananda? Oh yes, Ananda. And who are you, sweet friend?"

"I am Kisa's mother, Lasha, remember?" she replied, washing under my arms.

"Lasha?"

"You spent many a night at our house as a young girl."

I stared at Lasha as Kisa washed under my breasts, down my belly, and between my legs. "Lasha...Lasha?" Then I remembered. "Oh Lasha!" I cried as I put my arms around her neck.

By the time they finished cleaning me, I was back in the present.

"It's been so long," I exclaimed. "You look like a jewel."

"It is you who are one of the jewels of this world," Lasha replied.

"Remember..." I said, "remember when we dressed up in your clothes?"

"You two," Lasha shook her head at Kisa, then back at me. "You could be such devils." We all grinned. "Such impudence," she said lovingly. "You girls could sneak into anything, anywhere. More often than not, you ended up where you weren't supposed to be."

"But your clothes were so amazing!" Kisa exclaimed. "How did you wear all those things? We had to find out, didn't we?" she nodded at me.

"Yes. All that silk and jewelry; it felt so soft and glamorous." I rubbed my arm as if I was wearing one of her garments.

"You looked like two miniature sages who had accidentally fallen into a bundle of women's clothes," Lasha grinned. "You," she looked at me, "tried on my royal blue robe, the one with gold lining and trim. And one of my ruby necklaces was wrapped around your head like a metal turban." She looked at Kisa. "And you—you had my velvet slippers folded inside the top of my wedding dress, trying to look like a grown women. They were the funniest looking breasts I've ever seen."

"Let's dress up," I said. "I'll be you and you be me." I looked at Lasha.

"Not now, dear," Lasha said. "You already have on a beautiful gown and we wouldn't want to mess up your hair."

"Oh yes," I replied. Kisa turned away.

"Here," Lasha said, grabbing the brush from the table nearby, "let's comb out that beautiful hair of yours."

"OK," I smiled.

They helped me sit up in bed. Kisa held me against her shoulder while Lasha gently combed my tangled hair.

"Auntie Lasha," I said, "we'll be good, won't we, Kisa?" Kisa nodded.

"I know you will," Lasha replied.

"Can we stay up late and pretend?"

"Of course you can," she said, tears brimming in her eyes. "You can stay up as late as you want."

"We'll be quiet," I promised, "won't we, Kisa?"

Kisa took her time to answer, but finally said, "Yes. We'll be quiet. I promise."

"Come on, Kisa! Let's go." I tried getting out of bed, but they stopped me. They held on tightly, one on each side, as I tried to stand. My knees buckled and I almost fell. Somehow, they were able to keep me from falling. Next thing I knew, I was back in bed.

As we all lay panting from our exertions, Kisa at the bottom of the bed and Lasha sitting near the head, I said, "Kisa."

"Yes," she replied, still catching her breath.

"Maybe we could go play later. I'm a little tired right now."

"That sounds like a good idea," Lasha said, stroking my forehead. "Why not rest? You can play later."

"OK," I sighed, and closed my eyes. I felt Lasha getting up, opened my eyes, and grabbed her arm. "Auntie, where's Uncle? Is he with the king?"

Lasha seemed lost for words, then put her hand on me and said, "Yes, he's with Suddhodana. He'll be back tomorrow."

"Oh," I relaxed my grip. "I'd so love to see him. It's been such a long time."

Lasha looked at Kisa. They seemed confused.

"I'll tell him you wish to see him as soon as he returns," Lasha said.

"That would be lovely," I smiled. "There's something I need to tell him about the king's son, Siddhartha."

"What's that, dear?"

"It's a secret," I said softly. "I can only tell your husband."

"You can trust us," Kisa implored. "What is it?"

My eyes closed. The muscles on my face twitched involuntarily and then I relaxed, returning to another world of dreams.

Not sure if Yasodhara could hear them or not, Lasha motioned to her daughter to accompany her over to the table. They sat down, keeping an eye on Yasodhara in case she unexpectedly awoke and tried to get up again.

"Honey," Lasha said. "I'm so sorry."

Kisa shook her head in acknowledgment, tears flooding from the corners of her eyes.

"There's not much more we can do except keep her safe."

Kisa nodded. Lasha looked at her daughter, then back at Yasodhara.

"Almost nothing," she got up quickly. "Keep an eye on her." Kisa stood, wondering why her mother was suddenly headed towards the door. "I'll be right back," she explained. "I must talk to Sirimor."

As Kisa walked to the bed, she heard Sirimor urging the horses to move along. Her mother returned and sat beside her.

"What's going on?" Kisa asked.

"Something I should have done years ago."

Twenty-Two

Devadatta barreled in the door.

"I found him!" he told Chitra, who was in the middle of an argument with the cook.

She dismissed the cook. "Thank the gods," she said. "I knew you could do it."

"Where are they?" she exclaimed, after kissing him for his bravery and deserved boast.

"They're down at the stables," he replied gleefully, "unpacking their belongings."

Chitra ran outside. Devadatta sauntered after her, grinning profusely.

Halfway there she saw Rahula and several strangers walking towards the house.

As they met mid-way Devadatta started to make the introductions, but before he could say a word Chitra hugged Rahula and uncharacteristically cried on his chest.

"Auntie Chitra," Rahula held her close. "It's all right."

After a few moments Chitra stepped back and hugged Savarna, who was standing timidly next to her husband.

"You must be Savarna?"

Savarna nodded, thankful that Rahula had taught them enough of his native tongue to understand what was being said. Bodhi was hiding behind his mother, trying to avoid the attack of the crazy old lady who was carrying on.

Chitra exclaimed, "You are a beauty."

Savarna blushed a hundred shades.

Chitra couldn't contain herself and hugged Rahula once again, then saw Bodhi. "And who is this handsome young man?"

Rahula motioned for Bodhi to come out. Savarna moved to the side. As he stepped forward Rahula proudly said, "This is our son Bodhi."

Much to Bodhi's relief, Chitra didn't grab him or cry on his shoulder.

"It is a pleasure to meet you," she said, bowing respectfully. "Namasté."

Bodhi, caught off guard, stared for a moment, then returned her bow. "Namasté," he copied.

"I can't tell you how happy I am to see you," Chitra exclaimed. She dabbed at her eyes with a silk cloth, then, as if coming out of a deep sleep, realized there were others present. "Excuse me. My manners have escaped me." Turning to Ramu, Mirabi, and Jitaka she said, "Welcome."

"These are our friends," Rahula said. "Ramu, his daughter Mirabi, and her son Jitaka."

"It is a great honor and pleasure," Ramu bowed, holding his shoulder.

"The pleasure is ours," Chitra bowed back.

"We might not be here if it wasn't for Ramu," Rahula interceded, then turned to Devadatta, "and Uncle."

Ramu quickly deflected any praise. "Your husband and his men didn't arrive a second to soon."

Chitra looked at Devadatta for an explanation.

"I'll tell you later," he said, then faced their guests. "Come, you must be hungry."

As they made there way to the house Chitra put her arm around her nephew and held on all the way into the dining room.

After they had all washed and eaten more food than they usually ate in a month, they retired to the living room where Rahula told them about the kind-hearted people they had met on their journey, the heroics of Ramu, and their last-minute rescue by Devadatta. He also spoke about Savarna and Bodhi's bravery and his gratitude for their loving devotion.

Ramu said he couldn't be prouder of Rahula than if he was his own son.

After the guests were shown to their rooms and Bodhi fell asleep on Savarna's lap, Rahula asked, "How is she?"

"Not good," Devadatta replied.

"I must see her," Rahula said and started to stand.

His uncle put his hand on his shoulder. "Not now." Rahula sat back down. "Go tomorrow, when you're rested."

"Where is she?"

"On the other side of town," Chitra explained. "Remember Ananda?" Rahula nodded. "Ananda and Kisa are caring for her."

"She insisted," Devadatta said quickly.

"Yes," Rahula said thoughtfully. "That sounds like Mom. It's probably some run-down shack or cave, right?"

Chitra glanced at Devadatta, then replied, "It is a small hut but," she added, "it's not that bad."

Devadatta started to object, but caught himself and said, "No, it's not bad."

"Does she still talk about Father?"

"Sometimes," Devadatta grimaced, "but not much."

"Is she in pain?" Savarna asked quietly.

"No," Devadatta replied. "Every so often her chest hurts but it only lasts a few seconds."

"And how is Kisa? You say she stays there, too?"

"Yes," Chitra replied. "The darling girl is there every night. She's a godsend. I hate to think about what would happen without her."

Rahula smiled. "What a pair. That must be a crazy place with those two together."

Rahula looked towards Savarna. "They've been best friends since they were kids. Mom told me about some of the trouble they got into. You wouldn't believe what they've done." Savarna returned his smile.

"Are you sure it's best to wait until morning?" Rahula asked.

Devadatta looked quickly at Chitra. "Yes," he replied, with the assuring nod he received from his wife. "Yes, she'll be fine until then."

Devadatta picked up Bodhi, who laid his sleepy head on his great-uncle's shoulder. "Come," he said. "I'll show you to your rooms." Chitra hugged Rahula as they followed her husband to their plush rooms of slumber.

Twenty-Three

Ramu, Mirabi, and Jitaka bade farewell the next morning, respectfully declining their host's invitation to stay. They had to get home before the rains. "It should only take us three or four more days," Ramu predicted.

Rahula took Ramu aside and told him they would never forget his kindness and loyalty.

"Likewise," Ramu answered, putting his hand on Rahula's shoulder. "You are a brave man, not unlike your father."

"Papi!" Jitaka called to his grandfather. "Let's go!"

Before Rahula could reply Ramu, Mirabi, and Jitaka had climbed into the cart provided by Devadatta and pulled away.

Ramu shouted, "You should be proud!"

"What did he say?" Savarna asked.

"Nothing," he said, wondering how Ramu knew his father.

"Come," Devadatta said suddenly. "We must go."

As they walked through town, Rahula was amazed. Chitra and Savarna carried baskets of food and water, Bodhi wide-eyed by their side, tempted to bolt and explore.

"What's happened?" Rahula exclaimed, making his way through the hordes of merchants and shoppers lining the streets.

"Commerce," Devadatta replied proudly.

"I had no idea," Rahula said, as he was inadvertently jostled by several passersby. "This used to be a little backwater village with a few shops and fields."

"It's changed," Devadatta explained. "Up and down the Ganges towns are prospering; ordinary people are reaping the benefits." He turned to Rahula. "Surely you've seen other cities?"

"Yes, but I had no idea it had spread so far north."

"This is thousand size our village," Savarna told Chitra in broken Hindi.

"Really?" Chitra replied. "What is it like in Sri Lanka?

"Look, Mom, dancers!" Bodhi yelled, pointing at several women undulating in front of a dance hall. He started in their direction.

"Bodhi!" Savarna yelled. "Come back here." She grabbed his hand tightly. "You stay right here. I don't want you getting lost."

Bodhi pouted.

"It much much smaller," Savarna continued. "Everyone know everyone."

Chitra nodded.

"And clothes..." Savarna looked at the bright saris, turbans, and jewelry being worn by women and men, "our dress much simpler, less, what word...full of color."

Chitra laughed. "Not everyone thinks this is good," she explained. "A lot of religious fanatics think women should wear saris that cover us from head to toe."

"Fanatics?" Savarna puzzled. "What 'fanatic'?"

"You know," Chitra replied, "people who believe one way and think everyone else should believe the same."

"Like Buddha?" Savarna asked innocently. "Like Rahula father?"

"No! Not like Siddhartha. He never tried to convert or make people believe as he did." A few more thought-filled steps and Chitra asked, "So, you know about your father-in-law?" Savarna nodded. "I wasn't sure what Rahula had told you."

"He not talk about it. I find from other peoples."

"I had hoped things would be different."

"Why he and Devadatta anger at Buddha so?"

"It started when Siddhartha, the Buddha, left his sister two days after Rahula's birth. Devadatta never forgave him."

"He left?!"

"In the middle of the night, while they slept."

"Pray it not true!"

"It's true," Chitra said.

"And what Rahula? What father do make him so angry?"

"I don't know," Chitra tried explaining. "Devadatta told me Rahula told him what happened but he refused to let me know. He said it was between Rahula and Siddhartha and was not something for me to hear."

Savarna looked sadly at her husband and bowed her head. "Thank you, Chitra. Thank you for truth telling me."

She took Savarna's hand as they followed their husbands, praying beyond hope that something or somebody would miraculously free the men they loved from the pain they held so deeply.

Twenty-four

The sun was starting to nip at the morning fog. Ananda headed out the door to the well with his bucket.

"There is no need, Ananda," Chitra said, lifting a jug of water from her basket. "We brought some with us."

"Ananda?" Rahula asked. "Do you recognize me?"

Ananda gave a start and stared open-mouthed. He finally exclaimed, "Rahula?"

Rahula nodded. "I didn't think I'd ever see you again."

"Nor I you," Ananda admitted.

"I don't blame you."

"What?"

"I never blamed you. In fact..." Rahula said, "I am in your debt for the care you've been giving my mother."

"It is the least I can do. Your mother is a divine blessing."

"How is she?" Devadatta asked.

"Her effort and essence are strong but her body is falling away."

Rahula realized he hadn't introduced his family, which he proceeded to do, though with a heavy heart.

"It is a great honor," Ananda said, "to meet those who have nourished and cared for our dear Rahula while he was so far away from home."

Chitra came inside. They all followed. Ananda warned them that I was sleeping. I was lying on my side, hugging myself with both arms. My eyes were closed and my breathing labored.

Rahula broke down. Savarna and Bodhi stood close by. Devadatta's lip quivered. Chitra moved closer. As she leaned down, I opened my eyes and smiled.

Devadatta kneeled on the floor next to Chitra. "Good morning, sister."

Chitra smiled and whispered, "Good morning, Yasodhara."

Ananda stood in the back of the room observing from a distance.

"Sister," Devadatta said, "there's someone here to see you."

Rahula edged closer and knelt in front of me, his uncle's hand resting on his shoulder.

"Mother," Rahula said. "It's me," his hand touched my cheek, "your son."

I searched the face before me. "Rahula?"

"Yes," he said, tears streaming down his face, joining mine on the blanket. "It's me."

I reached out and touched his face. "It can't be. You're far away. It can't be."

"It's me." He put his arms around me, laid his face on my neck, and wept.

"I'm sorry," he cried. "I'm so sorry."

"Sorry?"

"I didn't plan on staying away so long."

"Where are you now, my joy?"

"I'm here with you."

"That's all that matters." Catching my breath, I rolled onto my back. Chitra and Savarna propped me up on some pillows.

"And who are you, sweet woman?" I wondered, as Savarna gave me some water.

"I am your son's wife."

"Ah, and do you have a name?"

"Savarna."

"Wonderful." I could see Rahula and Savarna's loving gaze. "The love you have for one another runs deep. I know that kind of love. Your father and I..."

"Mother, please!"

"He was so tender, so gentle and strong." Rahula turned away.

"But I wasn't enough...he was looking for something beyond ordinary love."

"Did find it he?" Savarna asked.

"Oh yes," I said, taking her hand in mine. "He found it and shared it with everyone."

Rahula and Devadatta swore under their breath.

"Rahula! Rahula!" My sight failed me.

"I'm right here, Mother." He grabbed my hand while Savarna held the other.

"Oh, Rahula. I've missed you so."

"And me you."

Bodhi went to his mother.

"Mother," Rahula said, "This is your grandson, Bodhi."

My sight returned. I saw a boy sitting before me. "Hello," he said timidly.

I couldn't stop staring. "You look like your grandfather." He squirmed. "It is a joy to meet you." He turned and asked his mother what I said.

"She said, it's good to meet you."

Bodhi turned around and said in the best Hindi he could manage, "Good to meet you, Grandpa."

We all laughed as Rahula said, "That's Grandma, not Grandpa."

"Sorry," Bodhi said. "Nice to meet you, Grandma."

"It is my honor." I felt tears streaming down my cheeks.

Bodhi's fear began to ease. He took a strand of my matted hair and said, "Your hair is long and gray like Grandma Chutharras."

Rahula translated and added, "Savarna's mother, his other grandma."

"I bet your grandma is wonderful, just like your mother."

Rahula told Bodhi what I said and his face lit up. "Oh yes," he said, speaking in Sinhalese. "She makes the best sweets in the world. And she's really fast for a grandma. When we play catch-me and you get a candy; she always grabs me before I can start. Even when she wins she gives me her sweets."

I could have sat and listened all day, even if I didn't know what he was saying. Rahula told him to slow down and not wear me out. He translated Bodhi's description of his grandma and everyone laughed.

My breath came rapidly as I grasped at thin air. Bodhi leaned back against his mother, wondering what he said that caused me to act so strange.

"It's OK," Ananda whispered, with the Sinhalese he picked up from his visits to Sri Lanka. "She's been doing this for a few days. It's part of the process."

"Is she dying?" I heard Bodhi ask.

"Yes," Ananda said, "she's dying."

"Oh," Bodhi said matter-of-factly, "that's why everyone is sad."

"Come back!" I yell at Siddhartha, who has been floating above me. "What? I don't understand." He throws me a small wad of cloth and then he's gone. I unfold the cloth and read the message. It says, "The bodhisattvas and Buddhas salute you and pay homage. You have gone beyond your mind and body and discovered your heart."

"Your son is here!" I shout, caring nothing about the state of my soul or the adoration of the Buddhas.

"He needs your heart." I crumple the cloth and throw it where he'd been. "Come back, you coward!"

My chest constricted in pain. I remembered Rahula was close by and reached out to find him. I could feel his hand and see his blurry face. I tried smiling so he wouldn't worry, but my eyes were heavy. I think I fell asleep again.

Devadatta was watching intently. His breathing was constricted, synchronized with Yasodhara's. He felt as helpless as a newborn. Wanting desperately to "do" something, but not knowing what to do, he went outside and yelled at the sun. "How could it be shining so brightly," he reasoned, "when I feel so dark?" He picked up some rocks and threw them at the banyan tree, then walked to the tree, tore off a branch, and started hitting the trunk with its amputated limb.

He sat down in the dirt, not giving an ox's ass whether he was ruining his fine silk garments. A cart rolled into the yard. The driver, who was dressed in fine attire, got out and helped someone who appeared to be a monk out of the back. "Why would a monk dressed in simple robes be riding in such luxury?" he wondered.

The monk spoke to the driver as he got back on the cart and yelled at the horses, "Move along!"

As the monk approached with a limp, he realized that it was not a man but a woman. Her head was shaved but her high cheekbones and brilliant eyes revealed an extraordinarily lovely woman whose age had done little to disguise her beauty.

She bowed to Devadatta and said, "Good morning, sir. My name is Ambapali. I have come to see my good friend and Dharma sister, Yasodhara."

Twenty-five

After a moment of awkward silence Ambapali inquired, "May I ask who this fine gentleman is standing before me?"

Devadatta crawled out of his stunned silence and said, in a low menacing tone, "I am Devadatta, Yasodhara's brother."

"It's a pleasure to meet you," she replied. "Yasodhara has spoken fondly of you and you're…"

"You have no right to be here!" he interrupted.

"I beg your pardon, brother, but I have every right."

"Have you no shame?" he said hoarsely. "Have you no decency or sense of honor?" She did not avert her gaze or her intention. "How do you have the nerve to come at a time like this? Who invited you?"

"Ananda," she replied softy, "and Yasodhara."

Devadatta groaned audibly and turned away. Ambapali gently touched his sleeve. "Don't you dare touch me," he hissed and turned again. She tugged at his sleeve again. He turned and raised his hand to strike. She did not move or flinch.

"If I have done anything to harm you or your family in word, deed, or thought, I humbly ask your forgiveness. Now is not the time for discord or ill-will."

He didn't have the energy to argue with this nun who, unlike most women (or men), didn't back down.

"My nephew and his family have just arrived. You're the last person he wants to see."

"Rahula's here?"

"They arrived last night. We just got here."

She was ecstatic. "Thank you! Thank you! What a blessing!"

Devadatta was puzzled.

"Ananda told me he'd written Rahula but I didn't think he would arrive in time." She hesitated. "He did get here in time, didn't he?"

"Barely."

"I am so grateful," she replied, "so grateful." After a moment of reflection she said, "How did he arrive so quickly?"

Devadatta's pride overwhelmed his anger. He told her about the rescue and how he and his men had sent the thieves running. He failed to mention that it was Ananda who had suggested he seek out Rahula.

"Devadatta," Ambapali said softly, bowing her head, "again, I ask your forgiveness. Any harm I have caused was the result of my ignorance and selfishness."

He hesitated. Suddenly, almost against his will, he placed his hand on Ambapali's soft shoulder and said, "It is I who has lived a life of ignorance."

Ambapali lifted her bowed head.

"Siddhartha was like a brother," he explained, tears visiting his eyes. "When Rahula told me about your liaison with his father, I blamed you."

Ambapali put her hand under Devadatta's elbow and led him to the corner of the yard in which he'd been sitting before her arrival.

He continued, "You were an easy target. After Siddhartha died, who was left to blame?" Ambapali understood. "I know that sounds crazy; he's the one who left us, not you; he coerced you to act improperly, I'm sure."

She knew that she initiated the contacts with Siddhartha, but most men assume it is they who are the pursuers and not the pursued.

"You were with him for years. I only saw him in big crowds. I resented your access." He looked at the hut. "I think Yasodhara became a nun to be close to him and got caught up in the whole religious thing."

Again, Ambapali realized there was no need to point out the inaccuracies in his assumption; it held some truth.

"Please," Ambapali said, starting to rise, "don't let me keep you from your obligations. I will go for a walk and return later."

"Stay. Rest," He waved at her to remain sitting. "I'll bring you nourishment and talk to Rahula."

She bowed so deeply her forehead touched the dirt.

"Thank you for sticking by Yasodhara," he said, standing. "You have come a long way. I apologize for my greeting. It was uncalled for."

"It was a natural reaction, by a brother who cares deeply about his sister and family."

Ambapali rejoiced. "Rahula has returned. What great blessings we have received." Even though she had never met Rahula in the flesh, Yasodhara spoke of him so often it felt like he was family. She remembered Yasodhara's confession during a winter retreat. She'd said that Rahula was all she lived for when Siddhartha left them.

"If anything happened to that boy," she said, "I don't think I could live."

"Surely," Ambapali replied, "you don't mean that."

"Oh yes," Yasodhara replied quickly, "without doubt."

"But," Ambapali reminded, "you know that attachment leads to suffering."

"Yes, I know, but he's my blood, my lifeline, my very foundation."

"You would carry on, even if you felt like dying. You would keep practicing the Dharma because you know it is the best medicine for broken hearts."

"Perhaps, but nobody knows until they have children. It is a powerful instinct, like an invisible tether that binds as strongly as you are bound to the Sangha."

Ambapali placed her hand on her stomach and said, "I had a son."

"Forgive me," Yasodhara apologized. "Where is he?"

"I do not know," she said sadly. "His body died when he was a baby. I've searched for years to discover him in another incarnation."

"How?" Yasodhara asked. "I mean…when?"

"I was young. It was part of the profession." She looked into Yasodhara's eyes. "You see? I do understand, even when I don't want to."

The sound of footsteps aroused Ambapali from her memories. Devadatta approached with a cup and bowl. He knelt and placed them before her. As he struggled to rise without losing his balance, he said, "I'm going to speak to Rahula."

She watched the proud old Brahmin re-enter the hut and prayed that his influence and reason would turn Rahula's heart.

Rahula burst forth, Devadatta and Ananda close behind. Chitra stayed inside to watch over Yasodhara. Savarna and Bodhi followed to the front door and watched from afar.

"Rahula!" Devadatta yelled. "Listen!"

Rahula stormed furiously towards Ambapali. Before he was even close he began shouting, "You stupid old woman!" Ambapali focused on her breath as Rahula knelt in front of her, his face fire-red. "You get out of here before I throw you out! Go back to your Buddhist tricks and take your begging bowl with you!" He knocked over the bowl of food Devadatta had set at her feet. "Do you hear me?" She didn't budge. "Are you deaf?" he shouted.

She opened her eyes and looked at the contortion of hate that appeared before her. "I am not your father," she said.

"You're damn right you're not my father!" Rahula screamed. "Damn right!"

He grabbed her by the arm, trying to force her to stand. Devadatta and Ananda restrained him.

"Let go," Devadatta said, staring into his nephew's eyes.

Rahula released his grip as Ananda helped Ambapali sit back down.

Rahula paced back and forth, mouthing obscenities, kicking dirt in her face, spitting accusations and curses like poisoned arrows.

"You are a whore!" he screamed, "nothing but a whore in the robe of a fanatic! You and my father! What a joke—two idiots who pretend to be holy, righteous, and good!" He kicked the poor tree that Devadatta had been beating on. "My mother has more understanding and love than you and all your nuns put together!"

"You're absolutely right," she agreed loudly.

"You and my father can burn in hell for all I care!" he continued. "You know how much he cared about humanity—he cared so much he left us two days after I was born! Two days!" he screamed in her face. "That's the kind of man you followed! That's the kind of man you slept with!"

"Yes," she agreed again, "that is the man I slept with and followed."

"You admit it!" He turned towards Ananda and Devadatta. "She admits it!"

"Yes," she said, "I admit it. I was young and foolish. Have you ever been young and done something foolish, Rahula? Have you ever done something you regretted the rest of your life and had to live with day in and day out? Have you ever asked and received forgiveness from the person you offended?"

"You knew he was married!"

"Yes."

"And you did it anyway?"

"Yes, Rahula, I did," she confessed. "Have you not known of others who went outside their marriage for love?"

"I'm not talking about others; I'm talking about my father, the great and noble Buddha, the man who didn't have time for his own family. The man who said he had transcended the desires of the world. The man who made love to a whore in the night and spoke about truth and compassion during the day. The man who belied everything he stood for!"

"You are right. Everything you have said is true. But," she caught his attention, "he was more than that, and so are you and I." Rahula stopped pacing.

"How can you say that?"

"After those first years together he denied my advances and taught me how to love without my body." Rahula waved his hand, trying to discount her nonsense, but kept listening. "His teachings transformed thousands with the truths he discovered."

"What truth is that?" Rahula scowled. "That one should leave their family, act like their son is nothing more than a hindrance, and abandon his wife like a used garment?"

"No," she replied with care. "He was right about how to observe ourselves, to see the cause of suffering and find a way to inner freedom, but he was wrong, dead wrong, about the need to leave one's family and loved ones behind." She paused, then continued. "When he started teaching there were few, if any, religious teachers that stayed at home. It's because of your father, when he admitted his error later in life, that thousands of householders joined the Sangha."

"He never admitted anything to me."

"How could he?" she replied. "You weren't here."

"Thank God mother didn't know about you. It would have killed her."

"It almost did."

"What?" Rahula screamed, inches from her face. Ananda started to intervene, but Ambapali raised her hand without Rahula noticing and waved him back.

"She found out years ago, not long after you left."

Rahula looked up at the sky as his tears fell to the ground. His legs shook. He sat with his head between his knees.

"The nuns were lying down to sleep, I don't remember where, when I sensed something in her had turned cold." She leaned closer to Rahula. "I don't know how she found out about your father and I, but she knew." Rahula looked up, his eyes red and tired. "Even though Siddhartha and I had not been lovers for over a year's time, I asked for her forgiveness."

Ambapali blinked slowly, then said, "Your mother was, as you said, more understanding and compassionate than I deserved. She said, 'It is not my place to forgive your actions; it is your karma. But you, as a woman, a friend, and a sister in the Dharma, I forgave a long time ago.'"

Placing her hand on Rahula's knee she said, "And now I must again ask for forgiveness. Will you forgive me for hurting you and your mother? Will you forgive the actions of a young, foolish girl who wanted nothing more than you did, to be close to Siddhartha?"

Savarna and Bodhi watched Rahula yelling at this old woman from the doorway. They had never seen him in such a state in all their lives. They couldn't understand why their husband/father was unleashing such hatred. Savarna caught a few words but could only fill in the rest with speculation.

Ananda, having noticed their confusion, told them the history of Ambapali and Rahula's father and translated some of the conversation.

"Don't be scared," he told Bodhi. "It looks frightening but it's long overdue. Only good will follow your father's release." Then, speaking to Savarna, "He is releasing the venom that has poisoned his heart for so long, is he not?"

She nodded, finally understanding the pain Rahula kept buried. "Thank you, Ananda. I have prayed to find a way to heal the sickness that has infected him for so long."

"Your prayers have been answered."

Ambapali lifted her hand from Rahula's knee. The sun's heat warmed her head as a breeze caressed her neck. She heard a child in the distance yelling at someone to play. The ground pressed on her anklebones. She could almost smell Rahula's fear. He was falling and didn't know where to land. She had shaken his mountain of hate. He had been pushed from the known into the unknown.

"You are not alone," she said.

Rahula stared into the eyes of the image he had hated for so long and all he saw reflected was love and understanding. There was no room for blame or accusation. He turned and saw Devadatta at his side, while Ananda stood with his wife and son. He was washed clean and hung out to dry but felt more alive than he had since childhood

Devadatta reached down and gave his nephew a hand. As he stood, Rahula said, "Uncle, come with me."

"Where are you going?" Savarna asked.

"We are going to get food and offerings for our guest," he grinned at Ambapali. "Perhaps she can forgive my cruelty."

Devadatta, grinning profusely, followed him out of the compound. As he came alongside his nephew, Rahula put his arm around his shoulder. "You were right, Uncle. She's not the demon I thought she was." Devadatta nodded. "In fact," Rahula exclaimed, "I'd say she's close to being a saint."

As soon as Devadatta and Rahula were out of sight, Savarna released Bodhi's hand and kneeled before Ambapali. She didn't know the words for gratitude in Hindi, so she bowed, took the old nun's hands in hers, and let her eyes and cries speak for her.

Bodhi stayed back from the women, watched the banyan tree, and thought about home. He missed his grandparents and his friends. He looked down the path that his father and great-uncle had gone and wondered what they were doing.

"Please," Ambapali said, extending her hand.

Savarna took her under one elbow and asked Bodhi to assist. He went to the old women and placed his hand under her other arm.

"Thank you," she said, gently removing everyone's hands. "I do have legs, be what they will." She nodded towards the house. "Let's go see that scoundrel who's caused so much trouble," she winked.

Twenty-Six

As Kisa and her mother approached the outskirts of Rajagaha, Rahula and Devadatta were headed the other direction.

"Devadatta?" exclaimed Kisa.

"Kisa!" he bellowed, as they met and bowed. "And this is your mother?"

"You remembered," Kisa replied.

"I could never forget the acquaintance of such a fine lady," Devadatta grinned. "Lasha, I believe?"

"Yes," Lasha replied. "We met years ago at the festival for King Suddhodana."

Kisa was distracted from the conversation, unable to take her eyes off the handsome young man standing behind Devadatta. He looked intimately familiar, but she couldn't fathom why.

"Forgive me," Devadatta stepped to the side, "this is my nephew, Rahula."

"Kisa?" Rahula said.

"Rahula!" she shouted, hugging him tightly and kissing his cheeks.

"I can't believe it!" Lasha added. "Last time I laid eyes on you, you were just coming into your own. Now look at you."

"Oh, Rahula," Kisa hugged him again. "You have no idea how much your mother longs to see you. We've all missed you."

Rahula's head bowed. Kisa stepped back. "You've seen her?"

"Yes."

"We're getting more provisions for an unexpected guest," Devadatta interrupted. "Chitra, Ananda, and Rahula's wife and son are there now."

"I can't wait to meet them," Kisa gushed.

"Who is the guest?" Lasha inquired.

"You'll never guess in a thousand ages," Devadatta grinned.

"Come on," Kisa exclaimed, her curiosity awakened, "who's there?"

"Come now," Lasha stated, "we aren't children. Who's there?"

Devadatta smiled at Rahula, then said, "Ambapali."

Mother and daughter's jaws dropped, not from news of the visitor, but from the cheerful composure of the two men they knew had hated her beyond reason.

Both men laughed.

"What's so funny?" Kisa asked.

"You should have seen your faces," Devadatta grinned. "Why are you so surprised? They have been friends for many, many years."

"Well, yes, of course," Lasha stammered, "but didn't you and Rahula, I mean what about your…"

Devadatta raised his hand. "The past is the past. If Yasodhara forgave her, can't we?"

"Of course," Kisa mumbled, "but…"

"We'll be back soon," Devadatta exclaimed, tugging on Rahula's sleeve. "There's no time to waste."

"See you there," Rahula waved.

"Yes," Lasha waved back. "Namasté."

They watched the two men walk arm in arm down the path, then looked at one another with delighted confusion.

"What on earth…?" Lasha exclaimed.

"I can't wait to hear about this," Kisa said. "Come on." She almost broke into a run.

"Hold on," Lasha called. "Wait for your old mother."

"Sorry, Mom," Kisa returned by her side. "I can't believe this, can you?"

"Yes, I can. When Yasodhara and Ambapali are together, anything is possible."

Twenty-Seven

Ananda entered and realized Yasodhara was halfway between here and there. He took Chitra aside and told her that her husband and Rahula would be back soon. He started to describe Rahula's interaction with Ambapali when Ambapali entered. Savarna and Bodhi followed.

"Can I wait outside for Dad?" Bodhi asked his mom.

"Sure, hon," she hushed, "but stay in the yard."

He darted outside, glad to be free of the overpowering emotions within his grandmother's home.

Ambapali walked with quiet deliberation to the bedside and gently sat on the edge. She instinctively noticed the curves, indentations, bumps, hair, and skin of her Dharma sister and reflected on mortality and one's fragile temporary existence.

"May you be happy, free from suffering, and at peace, my dear, dear friend," she whispered softly.

As if coming out of hibernation, I stretched my arms and fingers. My eyelids fluttered open and shut several times, then stayed wide open. My eyes rolled to the left, then to the right before Ambapali's sweet face appeared before me.

"...and you also," I replied.

She leaned closer. "What?"

"Peace, happy, no suffering," I puffed.

"Is it?" she asked.

"Oh yes," I beamed. "Oh yes."

As quickly as I had awoken I returned to sleep, or something akin to it.

Ambapali kissed Yasodhara on the forehead and sat back in contemplation. Ananda sat on the floor and did likewise. Chitra and Savarna bowed their heads in silence, praying their own private prayers to the divine presence that they believed would carry Yasodhara into the next world.

As Kisa and Lasha approached the yard, they saw a young boy at the entrance. When he saw them approaching, he retreated shyly and was soon out of sight. They entered the yard and saw him sitting by the banyan tree. He nodded, acknowledging their presence.

"Hello," Kisa said. "You must be Bodhi?" Hearing his name, he nodded. "I'm Kisa. This is my mother Lasha." He nodded again. "I've heard about you for years but had no idea you were such a big handsome boy."

Bodhi was lost. He nodded and smiled.

"Honey," Lasha said, "I don't think he understands."

"Oh," Kisa said, turning to Bodhi. "I'm sorry. Is your mother inside?"

He shook his head.

Pointing to herself, then her mother, then at Bodhi and the hut, Kisa asked again, "Is your mother inside?"

He understood and nodded.

"And your great aunt?" Kisa asked.

"Kisa," Lasha said, noting Bodhi's confusion and increasing discomfort, "let's just go in and see, OK?"

Kisa put her hand on her chest and pointed towards the hut. They left Bodhi, who was wondering if he was related to the two gesturing women, and went inside.

It was dark inside the musty dwelling and it took a few moments for their eyes to adjust. When their pupils were acclimated to the dim light they saw Ambapali and the others sitting with their eyes closed. Yasodhara's eyes were shut tight but her lips were moving.

Kisa tiptoed to the end of the bed. She was shocked at the changes from the previous day. Yasodhara was struggling with every breath, unsure if she wanted to take another.

Ambapali opened her eyes. "Kisa," she said quietly. "How wonderful to see you."

Kisa went to Ambapali and embraced the old nun.

"I'm so glad you arrived in time," Kisa whispered.

"As am I," Ambapali replied. "It's been too long." She turned and saw Lasha. "Isn't that your mother?"

"Yes," Kisa said. Lasha approached and bowed.

"Lasha, it is a great honor to see you and your daughter once again." She turned towards the others. "You know Chitra." They all bowed. "And this is Savarna, Rahula's wife." They bowed again.

"It is a pleasure, Savarna," Kisa grinned, as she and her mother tiptoed to the other side of the bed. "We have always desired to meet you."

Savarna didn't catch every word but felt their warm greeting.

"It is pleasure full to met you," she said in Hindi.

"We met your son," Kisa pointed outside. "Bodhi?"

"Yes, Bodhi our son."

"Rahula went with my husband into town," Chitra told Lasha. "They should be back soon."

"Yes," Lasha replied. "We met them on the path. They told us that Ambapali had arrived."

"You should have seen their faces," Kisa grinned. "I couldn't believe it," she spoke more softly. "I mean, you know," she nodded towards Ambapali, "they hated her so much. What happened?"

"I don't know," Chitra replied. "I was inside. I heard a lot of yelling but I didn't want to leave Yasodhara by herself. Ananda and Ambapali were outside."

"Whatever happened," Kisa said, glancing at Ambapali and Ananda, who appeared to have fallen asleep, "must have been something special. They were like two little boys who had just been given a thousand rupees to buy sweets."

They all grinned.

"Yes! Yes!" Yasodhara cried, staring at the roof.

"How can she still speak?" Kisa asked out loud. "She can hardly breathe."

"She's a warrior," Ambapali replied. "She finds strength and courage when there is none to be found."

As everyone sat down, Ambapali continued. "What happened with Rahula and Devadatta was nothing compared to Yasodhara."

As if on cue, drowning with every word, Yasodhara gargled, "Yes, my beloved. Yes."

"One time," Ambapali said, "when we were in Benares at the Ghaya Festival, we came upon a group of young Brahmins who were beating and kicking two defenseless untouchables for no apparent reason, other than their caste. They were laughing and shouting as if it were a game, grabbing the men's turbans, tearing off their shirts, and yelling at them to 'bark like the dogs you are!' When we saw them, I froze—couldn't budge an inch. I was afraid and thought there was nothing we could do."

She looked at Yasodhara. "She didn't hesitate. She walked calmly into the middle of the fray, picked up the shirts and turbans, handed them to the two men, and stood between them and the rich boys. At first the young Brahmins were shocked, but after a moment or two one of them approached Yasodhara and spit in her face, which even shocked his friends, since everyone could see that she was a nun. They all stepped back. 'This is none of your business!' the man who had soiled her screamed. 'Go worship whatever god you follow and leave us to the real things of the world.'

"Yasodhara wiped the spit from her face and not only didn't move away, but stepped closer to the angry young man. 'This is the god I follow,' she said. 'My religion is the world.' The young man smirked, turned his back to her, then, while smiling at his friends, drew his sword, swirled around, and brought it within a hair's breath of Yasodhara's neck. 'In the real world,' he hissed, 'people who interfere in other people's business end up dead!'"

Ambapali paused and looked at Savarna. "Your mother-in-law didn't flinch. She looked the young man in the eye and said, 'It would only increase your suffering, not mine.'"

Everyone looked at Yasodhara, envisioning the woman, whose useless body now lay gasping for breath, standing up to an angry young man with a sword at her throat. "I'll never forget the look on that boy's face. He didn't know whether to cry, run, or fight. After what seemed liked forever, he broke into a sarcastic grin, sheathed his sword, and said, 'I was only kidding, lady. You're not worth dirtying my blade.' Then he turned and yelled at his mates, 'Come on. Let this idiot play religious with these useless creatures!'"

After several minutes of awed silence Kisa said, "She never told me."

"There are a lot of things she's kept hidden," Ambapali replied.

"But," Kisa said, "I'm her best friend. She tells me everything."

"There are things she kept from me as well. She's never been prone to boasting or bragging. In fact," Ambapali paused, "she's let go of her self so much there were times I thought she would vanish into thin air."

"After Siddhartha left," Kisa said to herself, but loud enough for others to hear, "she cut off her hair, dressed in rough clothes, and slept on the ground. She did everything she heard that Siddhartha had done. We tried talking her out of it, told her how beautiful she was and how useless it was to ruin her good looks, but she wouldn't listen. After Rahula was grown and gone, we couldn't stop her from joining the Sangha."

"For years," Lasha added, "her step-mother couldn't look at her without crying. Yasodhara was compassionate and tried to teach her about attachment, suffering, and liberation, but all Pajapati could see was her beautiful child shaved bald, running around with a bunch of filthy-clothed radicals who begged for food." Lasha grinned. "She never gave up on her, though. She never threw her out of her heart. After several years Pajapati was finally able to look upon her daughter without sobbing." Lasha gazed at Yasodhara. "I'm glad she's not here now. This would surely break her heart."

"It breaks all of our hearts," Ambapali said.

The time between Yasodhara's breaths lengthened. The women cried.

"Papa!" Savarna heard her son and went to join him. It took her a moment to adjust to the brightness, even though the sun was beginning to make its descent. She could see Rahula and Devadatta carrying baskets and someone else on horseback. Bodhi ran to his father, who patted him on the head and handed him one of the smaller bags. Savarna joined them and bowed to her husband, who gave her a wink and a smile.

"Here," Devadatta exclaimed, taking a blanket out of one of the bags he had placed on the ground. "Let's set up by the tree. I'll get the others."

The man on horseback dismounted and joined Rahula, Savarna, and Bodhi while Devadatta went inside. He rubbed his eyes and walked to the bedside. After looking sadly upon his gasping sister, he said, "Kisa, Lasha, Ambapali, come with me." They looked bewildered. "Let's eat outside before the sun sets. We brought enough for hundreds."

"We can't leave her alone," Kisa exclaimed.

"She won't be," he said, helping Ambapali to her feet. "Ananda's here."

Ananda nodded, having been awoken from his nap. He stood to his full hunched height and went to the bedside.

"There's someone I'd like you to meet," Devadatta said, and walked Ambapali out the door. Kisa stared at her mother, who was as puzzled as she, and followed the others outside as Ananda kept vigil.

As they walked behind Devadatta and Ambapali, their eyes adjusting to the dimming light, Kisa couldn't see the man sitting on the blanket next to Rahula and Bodhi. As they got closer he came clearly into sight. She squinted, then blinked several times, thinking her eyes were playing tricks. By then her mother saw him as well. Kisa turned to her mother with total disbelief. Her mother returned her shocked gaze with a knowing grin.

"Father!" Kisa yelled, running to the old bearded man who quickly stood and embraced his daughter. Neither could stop the tears that followed. They held on tightly, afraid to ever let go again.

"How?" Kisa sobbed, "I mean why? Who told you? How did you know?"

"Your mother," he replied. "She sent a message saying if I didn't come to you and Yasodhara that she would leave me." He looked lovingly at Lasha, "And you know your mother. When she says something, she means it." He gazed at Kisa. "I couldn't live without her and I've been a fool to live without you."

They hugged again and wept.

"Will you ever forgive this old stubborn fool?" her father asked, Kisa's head upon his chest.

She looked into her father's brimming eyes. "Don't be silly. Where do you think I got my stubbornness from?"

"Come! Eat!" Devadatta hollered. "It will spoil by the time you three get around to it!"

As Kisa and her father and mother sat down with Devadatta, Ambapali, Rahula, Savarna, and Bodhi, Ananda appeared. He shuffled over to their blanket by the banyan tree, stood quietly, and looked past them at the orange and yellow horizon, tears dripping down his cheeks. They all looked up. Ananda went from face to face, acknowledging what they each knew. Yasodhara was dead.

The sky darkened as the first showers of the monsoons fell upon Rajagaha. Yasodhara, known far and wide as "the Buddha's wife," whose enlightened life of compassionate service touched thousands, would soon be relegated to a few drops of rain in the turbulent storms of recorded history.